Tilly and the Time Machine

Adrian Edmondson

illustrated by Danny Noble

PUFFIN

PUFFIN BOOKS

UK | USA | Canada | Ireland | Australia
India | New Zealand | South Africa

Puffin Books is part of the Penguin Random House group of companies
whose addresses can be found at global.penguinrandomhouse.com.

www.penguin.co.uk   www.puffin.co.uk   www.ladybird.co.uk

First published 2017
001

Set in Baskerville MT Std 12.5/20pt
Text design by Mandy Norman
Printed in Great Britian by Clays Ltd, St Ives plc

A CIP catalogue record for this book is available from the British Library

Hardback ISBN: 978–0–141–37243–3
Paperback ISBN: 978–0–141–37245–7

All correspondence to:
Puffin Books
Penguin Random House Children's
80 Strand, London WC2R 0RL

PUFFIN BOOKS

Tilly and the Time Machine

For Reuben, Betty, Eggy and Freya

CHAPTER

1

In the middle of the night there was a loud

explosion.

Tilly woke up with a start. At first she didn't know whether the bang she'd heard was part of a dream or something that had happened in real life.

She lay under her duvet looking this way and that, trying to see things in her dark bedroom. She really wanted to find out what had made the noise, but it was a freezing cold night and she really didn't want to get out of bed.

Suddenly, through the gap in her thin curtains,

she saw a shower of sparks, which lit up her tiny bedroom. It was as if someone had set off a large firework just outside her window. In the light of the sparks she could see Big Tedder and Mr Fluffybunny sitting on the shelf at the end of her bed. She could also see her uniform laid out on the chair behind the door, ready for school in the morning. And she could see the big photo of her with her mummy and her dad, which she kept in a frame on her bedside table. The photo had been taken in the kitchen downstairs, and they all looked very happy.

Tilly's house was what her dad called an old-fashioned 'two up, two down', which meant it had two rooms upstairs and two rooms downstairs. Though this wasn't strictly true: there was just her bedroom and her dad's bedroom upstairs, but downstairs there was a living room, a kitchen *and* a new bit of house that stuck out at the back, which was their bathroom.

There was another explosion, much smaller this time – more like a *crump* – followed by a different-coloured shower of sparks. Tilly sniffed the air with her tiny button of a nose. Could she smell burning? She would have to get up and investigate.

She slid out of bed, dragging the duvet with her, wrapping it round her like a lovely warm cloak. She shuffled across to the window and looked out.

The bathroom took up most of the space in the small yard at the back of the house, but her dad had still managed to squeeze a shed into the corner. This was where he did his 'experiments'. Tilly's dad was a scientist, and he loved inventing things. He used to invent things for the government, but he didn't work for them any more. In fact he didn't work for anyone any more, so he did all his inventing in the shed at home.

As she looked out of her bedroom window, Tilly could see her dad through the window of the shed. He was leaping up and down, grinning from ear to ear, and it looked like half his beard was on fire.

He turned and saw her, and immediately ran out of the shed, patting his beard to extinguish the flames.

'Tilly! Tilly! Come down and look at this! My machine – it's working!'

'Wow!' said Tilly excitedly, although she didn't really know what the machine was. But she moved away from the window, dropped her duvet on the floor and started towards the door.

'No time for the stairs!' shouted her dad. 'Just jump out of the window – I'll catch you!'

Tilly couldn't believe her ears. She ran back to the window and flung it open. 'Are you sure?' she shouted.

'Yes, of course! You're only small – I'll catch you!'

Tilly didn't like being called small. She was seven and a half, which in her opinion was quite big. But in the excitement of the moment she couldn't be bothered to argue. She scrambled on to the windowsill and looked down at her dad. His hair always stood on end as if he had just electrocuted himself, and he was smiling the big cheerful smile he always smiled. His beard was still smouldering, and she could see that one of the lenses of his thick black glasses was broken.

He held out his arms, ready to catch her.

Tilly stood there in her pyjamas. 'I-I'm f-frightened,' she stammered.

'Don't be such a scaredy-cat! It's hardly any distance at all – come on!'

Tilly knew that if her mummy was still alive she wouldn't let her do anything like this. Tilly missed her very much, but if there was any good side at all to her mummy dying it was that she could do the crazy stuff her dad let her do, like jumping out of windows.

'Life is for living, Tilly, my love,' shouted her dad. 'You only live once!'

'Here I come!' she shouted back, and she jumped off the ledge and landed safely in his arms.

'That's my girl. Come and look at this,' said her dad, carrying her quickly to the shed.

It was quite a small shed, but it was jam-packed with machinery. There were wires everywhere, as if the whole place was full of brightly coloured spaghetti. Lights blinked, wheels turned, and some things just shook and gurgled.

'What is it?' asked Tilly.

'It's a time machine!' said her dad. 'They told me I'd never get it to work, but finally it does! This evening I've already been to visit Admiral Nelson at the Battle of Trafalgar, and to the 1966 World Cup Final. You wouldn't believe it – I met the German goalkeeper Hans Tilkowski *and* Geoff Hurst! He scored three goals for England, although some people think his third goal didn't actually cross the line.'

These things didn't mean much to Tilly, but she could see that they impressed her dad.

'Come on,' he said, twiddling some dials and tapping away at his computer keyboard. 'Where

would you like to go? You can go anywhere
you like at any time in history – although at the
moment I can only manage to stay there for a
minute or two, then I pop straight back . . .'

'Anywhere at all?' asked Tilly.

'That's right, anywhere at all.'

'At any time I like?'

'At any time you like,' said her dad. 'You could
see a chariot race in ancient Rome, or travel with
the Pilgrim Fathers to America. Or – aren't you
doing a school project about Victorian England?
You could go there if you like.'

Tilly thought hard. She knew at once where
she wanted to go, but she was afraid to say, in case
her dad got upset.

'Come on,' he said enthusiastically. 'You
could see what life was really like for children
in Victorian times. You could even meet Queen
Victoria!' And he turned to his machine and
started typing in the details for Buckingham
Palace during the reign of Queen Victoria.

'I'd like to go back to my sixth birthday, when Mummy was still here,' said Tilly.

She didn't mean to say it aloud, but it just came out, because that's what she was thinking, and that's where she really wanted to go.

She knew her dad didn't like talking about her mummy, or the fact that she had died, because it made him sad.

He stopped what he was doing and sat very still for a moment. He sniffed hard a couple of times, and his eyes sparkled as if he was about to cry. Then he turned to Tilly. 'Are you sure you want to go back to your sixth birthday, my angel? Mummy was very poorly then, wasn't she?'

'But she was very smiley,' said Tilly. 'And that's when the photo was taken – the one I keep next to my bed; the one where everyone's laughing. It's the last photo of Mummy.'

Her dad took her in his arms and hugged her very tightly. 'Oh, Tilly, you're such a lovely little girl. Of course you want to see your mummy. Why didn't I think of that?'

One of her dad's arms was wrapped right round her head, and Tilly could hear the loud ticking of the watch he wore on his wrist.

She liked her dad's watch because her mummy had given it to him the Christmas before she died. On the back it had an engraving that read:

To my darling John,
I will love you for all time,
love Julia x

It was a very special watch. Not only did it have an extra-loud tick but it could tell you the day and the date, and what time sunrise and sunset were going to be. It also worked as a compass. Her dad was very pleased when he got it, and he always wore it.

Tilly also liked being hugged tightly, but after

a while she found it a bit difficult to breathe. Her face was pressed into her dad's jumper, and when she tried to speak her voice came out all muffled.

'Yuffoldenmeetootye,' she said through the thick wool.

'Pardon?' said her dad.

'Yuffoldenmeetootye,' said Tilly again.

Her dad stopped hugging her as tightly and looked at her. 'What did you say?' he asked.

'I said, "You're holding me too tight,"' said Tilly, and they both burst out laughing.

'Right, let's see what we can do!' her dad said, suddenly letting her go and turning back to his time machine. He was always happier doing things than talking about things.

'All I have to do is type in the details of your sixth birthday,' he said, merrily tapping away at his keyboard.

'The date.'

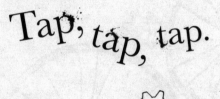

Tap, tap, tap.

'The exact address.'

Tap, tap, tap, tap, tap.

'And then we press this button here.'

Fixed to the time machine there was a big green button marked GO, and Tilly's dad pressed it.

'And off we go!' he said. 'Come on – no time to dawdle!'

He grabbed Tilly by the hand and took her into a small metal booth that was attached to the time machine by wires and tubes. He held her tight as the machine started to whizz and whirr.

Lights flashed,
wheels spun,

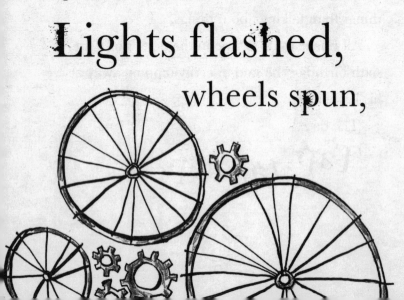

and the machine
started to make
a sound like an
aeroplane taking off,
and then . . . something
that looked a bit like a dustbin lid
fell off the top of a big cylinder in the middle of
the machine. There was a teeny-weeny explosion and
an even smaller spray of sparks, like the last
second of a sparkler before it dies. Then all the
lights faded and the machine turned itself off
with a loud

POP!

'Oh dear,' said Tilly's dad. 'That didn't sound good.'

The lights went off as well, and he got out a torch and started fiddling with the controls. Whatever he pressed didn't seem to make much difference. He scurried around the outside of the machine, checking connections and flicking switches, but nothing seemed to bring it back to life.

After ten minutes Tilly realized she was getting quite chilly. She was only wearing her pyjamas and, now that the heat of the machine had gone, the shed was cold and she could see her breath in the freezing night air.

'I think you'd better go back to bed, sweetheart. I'll try and get it fixed for the morning,' said her dad.

'I've got school in the morning,' she said.

'Well, I'll definitely have it up and running by home time,' he said. 'Go on – run along.' He gave her a big hug and a kiss, and ruffled her hair.

'School day tomorrow: you need your sleep, or you won't learn anything new and exciting.'

Tilly stepped out into the yard; her feet could feel the frost on the path as she tiptoed back to the house. She climbed the stairs to her bedroom and went to close her window. Looking out, she could see the light from her dad's torch in the shed flashing all over the place. There was obviously something seriously wrong with the machine.

She closed the window, drew the curtains, wrestled her duvet back on to the bed and climbed back in. Then she drifted off to sleep, wondering whether her feet would ever get warm again.

CHAPTER

When Tilly woke up the next morning, things seemed a bit strange. Firstly, she didn't normally wake up of her own accord. Usually her dad woke her. Secondly, it just didn't feel like early morning. When her dad had woken her yesterday, it was almost dark outside, but today it was bright and sunny.

She looked at the funny clock she'd been given the previous Christmas. The numbers were made of carrots, and a big floppy-eared rabbit pointed to the time. One of the rabbit's ears was pointing to the twelve, and his paw was pointing at the nine. It didn't take her long to work out that it was nine o'clock.

NINE O'CLOCK!

She was late for school. They must have overslept!

'Dad! Dad! We've overslept!' Tilly shouted as she jumped out of bed and quickly changed into her uniform. She ran out on to the landing and into her dad's room, but he wasn't there.

He must be making breakfast, she thought. So she ran downstairs into the kitchen, but he wasn't there either.

She saw that the back door was open a fraction. *He must be in the shed*, she thought. So she ran down the path and into the shed, but he wasn't there either.

The time machine was making a humming noise. Some of the lights were on, and occasionally one of the wheels would whirr a little, or one of the pipes would let out a bit of steam. It wasn't as lively as when Tilly had first seen it last night, but it was definitely more awake than when she'd left it and gone back to bed.

She looked at the computer screen. She could see the last three things her dad had typed into the machine: the date, time and address of her sixth birthday party.

She stood there, wondering what to do.

Gazing around, she became aware of a cupcake on the counter next to the computer. It looked very familiar. She examined it further. It wasn't any old cupcake; it was a cupcake from her sixth birthday – she was sure of it. It had blue swirly icing on top, into which was pressed a letter T made of chocolate. T for Tilly.

This was a cupcake from her birthday cupcake cake. Tilly had asked for it specially because her friend Jack had had one just like it. It was made of lots of cupcakes in lots of different colours, with big chocolate letters that spelled out **HAPPY BIRTHDAY TILLY**.

She remembered that on her sixth birthday her

dad had let her eat all the cupcakes that spelled out the word **HAPPY**, and that her mummy had been right – it had made her feel a bit queasy.

Tilly picked up the cupcake and had a close look at it. It was as fresh and tempting as it had been on the day of her sixth birthday. She looked around to see if anyone was watching because she knew she wasn't supposed to eat cupcakes for breakfast, and once she'd made sure she was all alone she took a big bite out of it. Yes, this was one of her birthday cupcake-cake cupcakes all right – she'd recognize it anywhere. She remembered her mummy making them all. They were absolutely delicious.

Once she'd finished the cupcake she didn't know quite what to do. She looked at the small metal booth where she'd sat with her dad when they'd tried to go back in time.

Tilly thought to herself, *If he's gone back in time again, this is where he'll reappear.* All she had to do was wait for him to come back.

She waited for a few moments.

Then she waited for quite a few more moments.

Then she sat down on her dad's stool and ate the cupcake crumbs that had fallen on to the counter.

She was pretty sure what had happened. Obviously her dad had gone back in time to her sixth birthday. He must have done it quite a few times, just to make sure the time machine worked properly, so he could take her there after school. In fact that was probably exactly what he was doing right now.

Tilly didn't know how long this might take. She decided that the best thing to do was go to school, let her dad sort it out and then he'd be able to take her to her sixth birthday afterwards.

She went back into the house and saw her lunch box on the kitchen table. She opened it – it was empty! She'd have to fill it herself.

Normally her dad would make her a sandwich, then put in some chopped-up pieces of carrot, a packet of raisins and a carton of juice.

Tilly looked in the fridge; it was full of weird jars and packets. She dragged a chair across the floor, climbed on to it and looked in the cupboard above the sink. It was full of boxes of rice, and jars of flour and sugar.

She wasn't sure where all the things to make a sandwich were. She knew that she wasn't allowed to use the sharp knives, so she definitely couldn't chop up carrots. And she couldn't find the packets of raisins. So she filled her lunch box with the chocolate digestive biscuits that were normally kept for a treat. She was sure her dad would understand.

Tilly went to the front door and put on her coat. She wondered whether she should clean her teeth. Her dad always made her clean her teeth before going to school. But she was already late, and her dad was always going on about 'getting an education', so she decided that school was more important than teeth. She didn't like cleaning her teeth anyway; it always took away the delicious taste of breakfast.

BREAKFAST! she suddenly thought. *I HAVEN'T HAD ANY PROPER BREAKFAST!* But she knew that if she stopped for breakfast now she'd make herself even later than she was already, so she decided she'd have a couple of chocolate digestive biscuits on the way to school, just to tide her over.

She picked up her book bag and her lunch box, opened the front door and was just about to slam it behind her when she remembered: *KEY!*

Suppose she got back and her dad was visiting Admiral Nelson in 1966 . . . If she didn't have a key she wouldn't be able to get back in. She looked on the key rack – her mummy's old front-door key was hanging there. She knew it was her mummy's because it was tied to the little woolly rabbit that Tilly had given her as a present.

Tilly put the key in her safest pocket and went off to school.

CHAPTER

By the time she got to school her face was covered in chocolate.

'Hello, Tilly Henderson,' said Mrs Higginbotham, the school secretary. She was a kind old lady who smelled of chicken soup and lavender. Her office was right next to the big entrance doors. When she saw Tilly, she came out to meet her. 'You're a bit late today, aren't you? Where's your father?'

Mrs Higginbotham looked out of the glass doors, up the path to the school gates. She could see a shock of black hair turning the corner and disappearing behind the wall. She imagined it was Tilly's father.

'I'm afraid we overslept because of my dad's time machine,' said Tilly.

'Oh, I know how easily that can happen – my alarm clock sometimes doesn't go off either. You've got a lot of chocolate around your mouth – and is that a bit of blue icing up there on your cheek?'

'It must be from my birthday cupcake cake,' said Tilly. 'The one my mummy made.'

Mrs Higginbotham knew that it wasn't Tilly's birthday today. She also knew what had happened to Tilly's mother, and that Tilly's father, who was a good man but a bit scatterbrained, was doing the best he could in the circumstances. Being a single parent wasn't easy, and he'd recently lost his job. Perhaps things had got a bit too much for him this morning.

'Let's get you cleaned up and into class,' said Mrs Higginbotham, taking hold of Tilly's rather sticky hand and leading her to the washrooms.

After Tilly had washed her hands and face, Mrs Higginbotham took her to her classroom. Tilly's teacher was called Miss Scarborough. She was quite small for a grown-up, with bright red hair and a cheerful freckly face. She always wore long flowery skirts, just like Tilly's mummy used to do.

As Tilly joined her best friend, Jack, at her usual table, she saw Mrs Higginbotham whispering something into Miss Scarborough's ear. Miss Scarborough turned to look at Tilly and gave her one of her extra-special smiles.

Tilly had a lovely morning.
At playtime, as a special treat,
Miss Scarborough let the
whole class play pirates, and
she sat next to Tilly when
she was explaining how to write
an important letter to someone.
She taught the class how to
write 'Dear Sir or Madam'
at the beginning, and 'Yours
faithfully' at the end; she told
them that if you'd forgotten to
say anything in the main part
of the letter, you could put
'PS' at the bottom and add
it there. And if you forgot
to put something in the PS bit,
you could write 'PPS' and add it there. And
if you forgot to put something in the 'PPS' bit,
you could write 'PPPS' and add it there. The
children thought that was very funny.

Tilly didn't even get into trouble when she opened her lunch box at lunchtime. All the other children had healthy lunches – cereal bars, sandwiches, yoghurts and fruit. Tilly's lunch box only had half a packet of chocolate digestives (she'd eaten the other half on the way to school).

Miss Scarborough did look a bit surprised when she saw what was in Tilly's lunch box, but instead of getting cross she just got everyone to share their lunches with Tilly. So Tilly had a big bite of Jack's cheese-and-ham sandwich, a not-so-big bite of a Marmite sandwich, a chicken drumstick, half a muesli bar, two grapes, three orange segments, a Babybel cheese, a stick of celery, some chopped-up carrot and three spoonfuls of yoghurt – one strawberry flavour, one vanilla flavour and one lychee flavour, which she didn't like very much. Miss Scarborough let her have one chocolate digestive to take away the taste of the lychees.

Tilly only started to worry when it got close to

home time. The teachers usually made sure that you didn't leave the school unless one of your parents was there. *This could get tricky*, she thought.

She didn't think her dad was doing anything wrong on purpose, but she imagined that if the teachers found out he hadn't actually brought her to school, he might get into trouble.

Tilly was only seven and a half, so she didn't understand everything grown-ups did, but she knew that lately her dad had been behaving rather strangely.

He'd recently received a very important letter in a brown envelope with HER MAJESTY'S GOVERNMENT RESEARCH CENTRE stamped on it. He didn't explain to her exactly what was written in the letter, but it had made him very angry.

"Wasting time"!'

he'd said, pointing to the letter. 'How can they call it "wasting time" when I've worked flat out for them for the last four and a half years. Not only do I slave away when I'm at the laboratory, but every evening I bring all the calculations home and work on them here. Sometimes I work all through the night, don't I? And I'm so close to the answer. So close! Well, if they have to "let me go" I'll just have to develop it myself. See how they like that!'

As far as Tilly could see, when someone 'let you go' it was quite nice. You could stay at home all day and you didn't have to go to work any more. Sometimes she wished the school would 'let her go'.

After school everyone stood in the playground waiting for their parents to pick them up. Miss Scarborough asked Tilly to stay close because she wanted to see her dad. Tilly looked anxiously at the school gates. Something told her that her dad wasn't going to pick her up today. And then he'd get into even more trouble. She'd have to think of something fast.

Jack's mum came into the playground. She wanted a word with Miss Scarborough. They got into one of those grown-up discussions when grown-ups hold their heads a bit higher and talk a bit more quietly, thinking that children can't hear them. Jack's mum was asking about 'Key Stage Two' and 'languages' and 'holidays in France' and 'private tutoring' and 'possibly changing schools'. This made Miss Scarborough look very serious, and they stood closer and closer so that their conversation was a little more private.

Tilly saw her chance.

'There's my dad! Bye, Miss Scarborough!' she said, rushing headlong out of the school gates.

Miss Scarborough didn't have time to see where Tilly's dad was in the crowd of parents outside the gates, or whether he was there at all, and Jack's mum was getting quite cross, so she had to pay attention to her and, before Miss Scarborough knew it, Tilly was out of sight.

CHAPTER

It wasn't far to Tilly's house. She turned right out of the gates and skipped along to the end of the road towards the High Street. The High Street was very busy, so Tilly decided to do 'spinning circles' all the way to the church.

'Spinning circles' was a special way of walking that Tilly's mummy had invented for getting through crowds of people: you take two steps forward, then spin all the way round, then take another two steps forward and spin round again, and so on, and so on. First you spin to the left and then you spin to the right – this stops you getting too dizzy. If you spread your arms out wide and sing a song at the top of your voice, it works even better.

Tilly sang a song called 'Shake Your Bum Around' that she and her mummy had made up. It was her mummy's favourite song. Whenever her mummy was feeling a bit down in the dumps because of her cancer treatment, Tilly sang 'Shake Your Bum Around' at the top of her voice. Her mummy always joined in, no matter how poorly she felt, and it always cheered her up.

So, as Tilly spun round and round, doing spinning circles along the pavement, she sang at the top of her voice:

'Shake your bum around,

Wiggle your bottom!

Shake it up and down,

Just shake your bum.

Shake it to the left,

Wiggle your bottom.

Shake it to the right,

My bum is fun!'

. . . and everyone jumped out of the way.

When she reached the church with the clock that didn't work any more she turned left and hopped on one leg as far as the scary closed-down factory. Then she turned right and hopped on her other leg into her own street, which was a cul-de-sac with a railway line at the bottom. There were houses on only one side of the street. On the other side the houses had been knocked down, and there was now just a pile of rubble with a tall fence around it. A sign on the fence said ACQUIRED FOR DEVELOPMENT.

Tilly's dad said that their house was an old-

fashioned 'terraced' house. It was in a line of houses that were all joined together. There were ten houses, and theirs was the last one in the row. The houses were quite old, and some of them had weeds growing out between the dirty bricks.

It was easy to spot their house because it was the only one that was lived in. The other nine houses had big sheets of metal fixed over the windows and doors. Her dad said this was to stop 'squatters', though why people would want to squat down all day in an old house, Tilly couldn't imagine.

She thought the metal sheets made the houses look as if they were wearing blindfolds. Her house had two lovely windows upstairs, a lovely window downstairs and a cherry-red front door. It looked like a very friendly lopsided face, with a mouth that was wearing bright red lipstick.

She rummaged around in her pocket, found her mummy's old front-door key and let herself in, carefully closing the door behind her.

'Dad!' she called out, but she didn't expect him to be there, and he wasn't. She went through the kitchen, out of the back door, along the path and into the shed. The time machine was looking even perkier than it had before she left to go to school. All its lights were blinking, and the motors were making a kind of purring sound, like a ginormous cat.

On one side of the computer Tilly saw some very important-looking plans. She thought they might be the plans for the time machine, but then she saw that they were labelled

REMOTE BOMB-DISPOSAL DEVICE. The device looked a bit like a robotic dog.

On the other side of the computer there were lots of bits of paper that had been scribbled on. Tilly recognized the scribble – it was her dad's handwriting. She tried to read it. It was hard enough reading the last birthday card her dad had given her, but this was super tough. After a few minutes of trying really hard she could just about make out a few bits of the sentences:

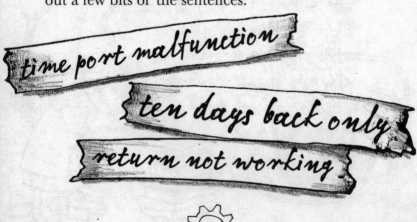

time port malfunction

ten days back only

return not working

The rest was just a lot of maths. Tilly had done adding, subtracting, dividing and multiplication, but these sums looked like someone had jumbled up a load of numbers and then forgotten where they all went.

She looked at the computer to see where her dad had been trying to go. She was quite good at scrolling up and down because he sometimes let her play a game where she had to make a frog cross the road without getting run over.

These were the places he had been trying to go:

Tilly's 6th birthday
Pink Floyd, Dark Side of the Moon, 1972,
    Rainbow Theatre
Tilly's school
Tilly's school project
HM Government Research Centre
Reprogramming, test run, after error
    code 404
Test run

She recognized 'Tilly's 6th birthday'. She also recognized 'Tilly's school', and she remembered how, that morning, Mrs Higginbotham had looked out at the gates and seen what she thought was Tilly's dad disappearing behind the wall; perhaps that actually *had been* her dad! Maybe he'd used the time machine to make sure she got to school safely.

HM Government Research Centre was where her dad used to work. Tilly couldn't think why he would want to go back there – whenever he talked about it he said he hated it and everyone who worked there. 'They're all complete idiots!' he always said.

Tilly stared at the machine; it looked so inviting, as if it wanted her to have a go. She turned round to make sure no one was watching, then typed in the date, the time and the exact address of her sixth birthday party, and pressed the big green button marked GO.

She jumped into the small metal booth and

waited. She was quite
scared, but also very
excited. Any moment
now she might see
her mummy again!
She took off her coat,
then quickly brushed her
school jumper to get any
crumbs off it and tried to
make her hair look tidy.

The machine made lots of noises –

some whoops,

some whirrs,

some whines

and a couple of beeps

– but then settled down to purring again, just

like it was doing before. Tilly sat in the booth, wondering if it was working or whether it had stopped.

When she was sure nothing was going to happen she crept back to the computer. A big message was flashing across the screen. It said:

Error code 404
Temporary fault in wormhole
    configuration
Coordinates too far into the past

Tilly's eyes scanned the machine. She couldn't see any worms anywhere. Did the machine run on worms?

The cor-somethings were too far into the past . . . Perhaps the machine was a bit broken and couldn't take her as far back as her sixth birthday any more? It was quite a long time ago – she was seven and a half now.

Tilly thought for a minute and wished there

was another cupcake sitting on the counter. Another cupcake would give her some brain energy, she thought. She spied the empty cupcake case, and with her fingernail she scraped out some of the crumbs that were still stuck to the bottom and put them in her mouth. They tasted delicious, and almost immediately she had an idea! *I'll test the machine*, she thought. *I'll see if it will go just a little bit back in time.*

She tapped in the time she normally got to school, today's date and the address of the school, which she knew off by heart. She pressed the big green button and went back into the small metal booth.

The machine whooped and whirred and zinged, lights flashed, there was a burst of steam

and suddenly Tilly was standing in the school
playground with all the other children, and
Mrs Higginbotham was ringing the handbell
and telling them all to line up in their classes,
ready to go in.

Tilly couldn't believe her eyes.

'What's the matter with you?' said Jack,
who was standing next to her. 'You look very
surprised.'

'I can't believe I'm here,' said Tilly.

'I know – it's horrible, isn't it? Still, it's the last day of school before half-term. We don't have to come next week. Me and my family are going to the Dong-di-doyne in France. Are you going away on holiday?'

'I think we might be going to the dark side of the moon,' said Tilly.

'Why do you want to go there?' asked Jack. 'If it's dark, you won't be able to see anything. You should go to the light side of the moon.'

Mrs Higginbotham blew her whistle and all the classes filed into their classrooms. Tilly and Jack stood at their table, and Miss Scarborough explained that today they would be doing more work on their project about the Victorians.

Tilly quite liked the Victorians. Her table had been finding out about the food the Victorians used to eat. Tilly was very pleased when Miss Scarborough gave her a special task: to find out all about something called 'Afternoon Tea'.

In Victorian times rich people used to have a big

breakfast in the morning, a very small lunch, and then they wouldn't eat again until they had a big dinner at eight or nine o'clock in the evening. A rich lady called the Duchess of Bedford found she got a bit hungry in the long hours between the small lunch and dinner, so she invented afternoon tea.

Afternoon tea wasn't just a cup of tea in the afternoon. Afternoon tea was a cup of tea and lots of other things. It was all served on a pretty stand, which was made of three plates fixed one above the other, with big gaps in between.

To show what afternoon tea was like, Tilly drew a picture of the three plates fixed one above the other, showing exactly what would have been on each one.

On the top plate she put 'finger sandwiches'. These weren't sandwiches with fingers inside, as she'd first imagined. They were sandwiches with the crusts cut off that were cut quite long and thin, so they looked a bit like long white fingers.

Tilly drew some with a filling of yellow and green; these were egg-and-cress sandwiches, which

48

she really loved. Her mummy had often made her egg-and-cress sandwiches. She drew some with a brown filling for beef, and some with a green filling for cucumbers. She decided not to draw the smoked-salmon one Miss Scarborough had told her about because she didn't really like smoked salmon – it was a bit slimy.

On the second plate she drew small individual tarts with real fruit on top, miniature Victoria sponge cakes, shortbread biscuits and lots of brightly coloured macaroons. There was nothing on the second plate that Tilly didn't like. She would have quite happily scoffed the lot.

On the bottom plate she drew freshly baked scones with little pots of cream and strawberry jam. Oh, the very thought of the cream melting into those warm scones made Tilly's mouth water. In fact her mouth watered so much that a little bit of dribble escaped from the corner and landed on the drawing. Tilly hoped that no one had noticed and quickly used some paint to cover the mark the

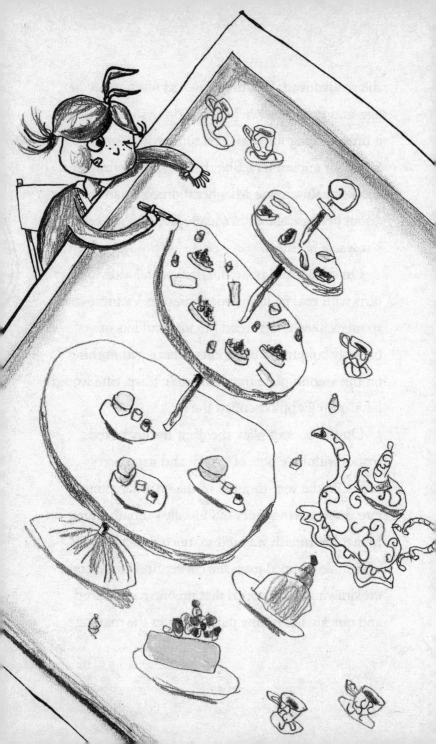

dribble had made. Luckily she'd dribbled on to the pot of strawberry jam.

Tilly thought the only thing that could have made afternoon tea any better would be party sausages on sticks, but Miss Scarborough said that they didn't have party sausages on sticks in the Victorian era. This made Tilly like the Victorians a little less than she had before.

Jack, who was sitting next to her, had been finding out what Queen Victoria used to eat. He discovered that she loved to eat meat more than anything else, but the funniest thing was that she used to eat her food extremely quickly. She ate quite a lot, and she really gobbled it down. And as soon as *she* had finished eating, she expected the servants to clear *everyone's* plate away, even if they hadn't finished! It sounded very funny.

There were several pictures of Queen Victoria on the classroom wall. In each one she was wearing black clothes. All her clothes were black, and she never seemed to be smiling.

'Why is she wearing black clothes and not smiling?' Tilly asked Miss Scarborough.

'Because her husband, Prince Albert, had died,' said Miss Scarborough.

'When my mummy died, my dad wore black clothes,' said Tilly. 'But my aunty Helen said he was wrong, and that we should all wear our most colourful party clothes because that's what my mummy would have wanted.'

But Tilly didn't actually get to the end of her sentence. She'd only just managed to say, 'But my aunty Helen said he was wrong, and that we should all wear our most colourful party clothes because –' when suddenly she found herself back in the booth in the shed. She had travelled forward through time to where she'd been when she pressed the big green button marked GO.

Well, that was a very odd experience, Tilly thought to herself.

She felt a rumble in her tummy. All the time travel and talk of afternoon tea were making her peckish. She went back into the kitchen to find something to eat. She wasn't in a massive hurry, like she'd been before school this morning, so she had time to have a good rummage around. There wasn't much in the way of afternoon tea in the cupboards.

Ten minutes later she sat down at the kitchen table with what she had found. It was a slab of raw jelly, straight from the packet – before it had been made into normal jelly by mixing it with boiling water and letting it set in the fridge. Sometimes when her mummy was making jelly she would let Tilly have a single raw cube.

Tilly loved it – it tasted like concentrated jelly –
and now she had a whole packet all to herself. She
put the raw jelly on the table and cut a chunk off
with a spoon. She had just put it in her mouth
when there was a knock at the front door.

Tilly got off her chair and went down the
hall. She opened the flap where the letters came
through and peered out. She could see two
raincoats and two pairs of hands. One of the
hands was holding an important-looking briefcase
with a small picture of a crown printed on it in
gold.

'Hello,' she said. Well, she didn't actually say
'Hello'. What she actually said was 'Erroow'
because her mouth was full of jelly. She knew
it was rude to talk with her mouth full, so she
swallowed the lump of jelly in one go and then
said 'Hello' properly.

The two people crouched down to look
through the letter box. They were both men of
about her dad's age, though they were much more

smartly dressed. They both wore suits and ties, and one of them had a very neat moustache.

'Hello, little girl,' said the man with the moustache.

'I'm not little. I'm seven and a half, and I'm average height for my age,' said Tilly.

The man smiled. 'I'm sorry, I couldn't quite tell how tall you were through the door. Is your father in?'

'No.'

'Do you know where he is?'

Tilly wondered if her dad would get into trouble if the men found out that she was all alone in the house, so she told them a little fib that was sort of half true, so it didn't feel like a fib.

'He's gone for a run,' she said.

'Do you think we could come in and wait for him? We're from your father's work,' said the man, getting a little piece of card out of his pocket and handing it to Tilly through the letter box.

Tilly read the card. It said:

HER MAJESTY'S GOVERNMENT RESEARCH CENTRE
Sir Digby Snottington
HEAD OF DEPARTMENT

'Oh,' she said. 'Are you one of the complete idiots?'

'I beg your pardon?'

'My dad says that all the people at work are complete idiots.'

'Oh, he does, does he?' said the man with the moustache, looking rather cross.

'Yes. And, anyway, my dad doesn't actually work there any more – they had to let him go.'

The man with the moustache suddenly looked as if he was sweating, even though it wasn't a hot day. 'Yes,' he said. 'I'm afraid there's been a little misunderstanding. Are you sure we can't come in and wait for him?'

'Absolutely sure. My mummy said you should never open the door to strangers.'

'Oh. Is your mummy in?'

'No, she's dead,' said Tilly. 'She's in a box in a hole in the ground near the church, all covered up with mud and dirt.'

The man with the moustache didn't know what to say. He looked like he'd suddenly swallowed a whole hard-boiled egg in one go. He and the other man stood up and whispered something to each other. Then the man with the moustache bent down to look at Tilly through the letter-box flap and said, 'We'll be back later.'

CHAPTER

As soon as the men had gone, Tilly
went back into the kitchen and had
two more cubes of raw jelly.

She decided it would be
best not to use the time
machine again until
her dad came back.
She was afraid that
if she did she might
break it, and then he might never be able
to get back. So – taking another couple of jelly
cubes with her – she went out to the shed and left
a note for her dad on the counter. It said:

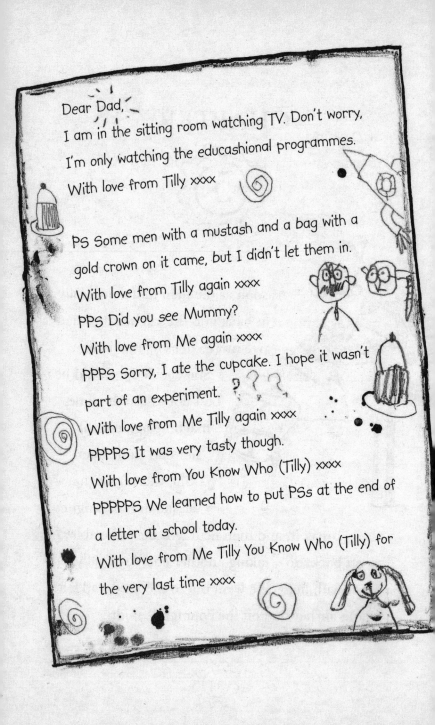

Dear Dad,

I am in the sitting room watching TV. Don't worry, I'm only watching the educashional programmes.

With love from Tilly xxxx

PS Some men with a mustash and a bag with a gold crown on it came, but I didn't let them in.

With love from Tilly again xxxx

PPS Did you see Mummy?

With love from Me again xxxx

PPPS Sorry, I ate the cupcake. I hope it wasn't part of an experiment. ???

With love from Me Tilly again xxxx

PPPPS It was very tasty though.

With love from You Know Who (Tilly) xxxx

PPPPPS We learned how to put PSs at the end of a letter at school today.

With love from Me Tilly You Know Who (Tilly) for the very last time xxxx

She went back into the house and had three more cubes of raw jelly. They took quite a lot of chewing, but she stuck at it and eventually managed to swallow them down. Now there were only four cubes left, and she didn't want to seem a greedy pig and eat the whole packet, so she had just one more cube and left the rest on the table.

She changed out of her school uniform, went into the sitting room and turned on the telly. She quickly checked that her dad hadn't come back, then watched all of *The One Show* and all of *EastEnders*. They were her mummy's favourite programmes. It was fun to watch them without her dad saying, 'This is rubbish – it'll rot your brain,' every five minutes.

After *EastEnders* finished, Tilly felt a bit hungry again. She knew she wasn't allowed to use the cooker, so she carefully opened a tin of baked beans with tiny sausages, and ate them cold out of the tin. For pudding she had a Fruit Corner, a

Müller Rice, the last three cubes of jelly and two
handfuls of Choc Pops. She felt quite full.

She watched the DVD of *Frozen*, singing along
with all the songs.

Tilly got quite snuggly on the sofa and pulled
the cushions over her like a big thick blanket.
When the DVD stopped, the telly programmes
came back on automatically. It was *The News*. She
didn't normally like *The News*, but she couldn't be
bothered to move because she was so warm and
comfortable.

The big story on *The News* was about Her Majesty's Government Research Centre! Tilly was quite surprised and listened carefully.

The news lady said that earlier that day the scientists from the research centre had invited lots of people to look at their new bomb-disposal device. They showed the device. It was the thing from the plans! The plans next to the computer in the shed – the thing that looked a little bit like a robot dog. Tilly paid even more attention to the TV than she had before. She'd never been as interested in *The News*.

Then she saw the man with the moustache on the TV; the man who had been talking to her through the letter box that very afternoon! Tilly couldn't believe her eyes.

He told the news lady that this new robotic bomb-disposal unit was a breakthrough in modern science. He said it could actually sniff out different types of bomb and then work out ways of making them safe.

There were a lot of scientists in white coats at the research centre. They all looked very pleased with themselves. They put a small pretend bomb under a car and turned on the robot dog. It was supposed to find the bomb by its sense of smell and work out how to stop it going off.

What it did instead made Tilly laugh and laugh

and laugh. The little robot dog went over to the car, but instead of sniffing the bomb it walked round the car on to the pavement and starting sniffing a lamp post instead. Then it lifted one leg and did a wee on the lamp post!

The scientists in white coats looked very shocked. They watched with open mouths as the

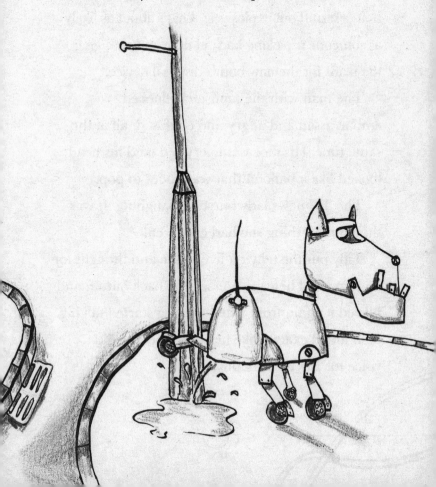

robot dog scampered off, picked up a stick and ran back to the news reporter. It dropped the stick at the reporter's feet, looking as if it wanted to play fetch.

Then . . . it talked!

In a little doggy voice that sounded a bit like Tilly's dad doing a funny voice, it said, 'A robot dog that can sniff out explosives? That's about as likely as someone travelling back in time and changing the plans for the new bomb-disposal device!'

The man with the moustache looked embarrassed and angry and confused, all at the same time. His face went very red, and his head looked like a balloon that was about to pop.

The TV news lady burst out laughing. It was the funniest thing she had ever seen!

Tilly put the telly on live pause and thought for a moment. Then she pressed the back button and played it again from when the dog started talking. It sounded exactly like her dad when he did a voice for Mr Fluffybunny.

She wound it back and played it for a third time. 'A robot dog that can sniff out explosives? That's about as likely as someone travelling back in time and changing the plans for the new bomb-disposal device!'

It *was* her dad's voice!

She was sure of it. That's why the dog was talking about travelling back in time!

Tilly remembered the list of places her dad had been to in the time machine. The Government Research Centre was definitely one of them.

She thought really hard about it all and started putting two and two together: her dad must have gone back in time and done something to the robot dog to make it do silly things instead of what it was supposed to do. He must have done it on purpose, to make the scientists and the man with the moustache look stupid! What a clever man her dad was.

Unfortunately, remembering how clever he was

made Tilly remember that he wasn't there.

She wasn't exactly scared and she wasn't exactly lonely, but she was slightly worried. She knew it was way past her bedtime, but she'd never put herself to bed before.

Usually her dad gave her a cup of cocoa, then he made her have a bath, then he made her clean her teeth, and then she got into bed and he read her a story. After story time Tilly always kissed the photo of her with her mummy and her dad, then her dad gave her a big hug, and then he turned out the light and left.

She wasn't quite sure whether she was allowed to use the kettle on her own, so she couldn't make cocoa.

She inspected her arms and legs and thought to herself, *I'm not actually very dirty, so I don't think I need a bath.*

She did clean her teeth because she hadn't cleaned them since the night before and they felt a bit furry. As she brushed up and down and from side to side, she thought to herself, *What a good girl I am. I deserve a gold star for being this good.* So she went into the kitchen and added a star to the star chart they kept on the fridge door. *It's what Dad would have done,* she told herself.

She changed into her pyjamas, got into bed and picked up the storybook that her dad had been reading to her. It was about a faraway time when there were people with big hairy feet called hobbits who were on a secret mission to take a ring to a cave, or something. Tilly tried reading it to herself. She was a good reader for her age, but the story seemed much better when her dad read it out loud, so after two sentences she gave up.

She kissed the photo of her with her mummy and her dad, turned off the bedside light and settled down to go to sleep.

CHAPTER

Suddenly she had a very funny feeling. It was one of those times when you feel half excited and half discombobulated, and you're not quite sure if you're happy or sad, or about to be sick.

Something was different!

What was it?

Tilly stared into the dark, trying to think. It was the photo! There was something different about the photo!

She turned on the bedside light and looked at it. The photo showed her, her mummy and her dad all sitting in the kitchen. It had been taken on the morning of her sixth birthday, before her friends arrived for the party. It wasn't the best photo in the world – most of it was taken up by the huge white fridge behind them – but she liked it because they all looked so happy, and because it was the last photo that had been taken of her mummy before she died.

What was different?

And then she saw it. It was the fridge!

The fridge normally had lots of things on it: magnetic letters she used for spelling practice, paintings she'd brought back from school, a magnet of a ladybird playing tennis, another of the Eiffel Tower, her star chart and the shopping-list thingy that had a pencil on a string hanging down from it.

But, looking at it now, Tilly saw that those things had been cleared away, and there was just a message written in magnetic letters across the whole fridge.

The message read:

tilly help
stuck in time
check machine
reset passcode
mydar lingju lia
look out for spies
love dad x

Tilly studied the message. The first thing she thought was that if Miss Scarborough saw this, she'd give her dad a telling-off because his punctuation was terrible.

Then she remembered that there weren't any commas or full stops or capitals in the set of magnetic letters, so she let him off.

She quickly put on her slippers and went downstairs. She took the framed photograph with her so that she could see what her dad had written. She thought this was quite a clever thing to do, and wondered whether she should give herself another star there and then, but decided there wasn't enough time to stop and do that.

She went out into the yard, and she was just walking down the short path when she heard gruff whispering voices coming from behind the wall – the wall that was behind the shed. She could hear two distinct voices. The first one sounded very stupid and the second one sounded just slightly stupid.

'This is the house, is it?' said the very stupid-sounding voice.

'Yeah, he says the machine's in a shed just behind this wall,' said the only slightly stupid-sounding voice.

'And we just got to smash it up, right?'

'No, no, no! The bloke with the moustache

wants it in one piece! If we breaks it, we don't get paid!'

'All right, all right, keep your hair on! Right, give us a leg up and I'll have a quick shufti.'

Tilly heard some grunting – then suddenly a rough pair of hands came up over the wall, followed by the face of a very mean-looking man. Although, to be honest, Tilly couldn't see very much of his face: he was wearing a black bobble hat, which he'd pulled right down over his eyebrows, and his black jacket, which had an elasticated collar, was zipped right up over his chin and mouth. All Tilly could see was his big crooked nose and two dark, evil eyes that stared at her in surprise.

'Flaming Nora, Harry! There's a kid here!' he said. 'What you doing up at this time of night?'

Tilly didn't know what to say. The mean-looking man was climbing right up on to the wall now and was turning round to give the one called Harry a hand up too. But Harry was obviously a lot fatter and heavier than the mean-looking man because it was proving quite a struggle to lift him up.

Tilly seized her moment. She ran into the shed, shut the door behind her and sat down at the computer.

She knew her dad wanted her to reset a code or something, but she had no idea how to do it.

She looked at the photo in the frame and at the message written on the fridge – and the message had changed!

Everything else was exactly the same: she was still smiling her funny smile with two teeth missing, her mummy was holding her tight and laughing, and her dad was pulling his funny squinty-eyed face – the one he always pulled for photos – *but* the message on the fridge now said:

press f9

screen says reset
press y for yes

type password

mydar lingju lia

Tilly could hear the men on the roof of the shed now. They were clomping about like a pair of elephants.

She pressed F9 on the computer keyboard; it was one of the keys at the top. The screen came up with a message that read RESET PROGRAM? Tilly pressed Y for yes, and the screen came up with a box marked PASSWORD.

Out of the window she could see one of the men's legs dangling down from the roof.

She typed in the password as carefully as she could: mydar lingju lia. As soon as she put it in, the time machine began to come back to life. Everything started spinning and whirring, lights were flashing and there was a very satisfying electric hum.

Tilly heard a sharp tapping on the window and looked round. The mean-looking man had jumped down from the shed roof and was now staring at her through the glass.

'What you doing? Leave that alone!' he shouted through the window, but, unluckily for him, just at that moment Harry, who really was very large indeed, fell off the roof and knocked him to the ground.

Tilly turned back to the computer. Her
only escape was to disappear into the past. But
where should she go? Somehow she had to stop
these two men from stealing the time machine,
otherwise her dad might never get home.

Quick as a flash she typed in today's date
and her home address, then she set the time for
exactly two hours ago.

As she pressed the big green button marked
GO she could see the men getting to their feet and
heading towards the door of the shed.

She ran into the small metal booth and sat
down.

The men burst through the door . . .

But, just as they tried to grab her, she

disappeared!

CHAPTER

Tilly immediately found herself back on the sofa, watching the end of *EastEnders*.

The first thing she thought to herself was,
I wonder if I've had my tea yet.

She went into the kitchen and saw that the tin of beans with sausages, the Fruit Corner, the Müller Rice, the three cubes of raw jelly and the box of Choc Pops were still there. So she sat down at the kitchen table and ate them all over again. They were yummy.

When she'd finished, she half thought about going back in time to ten minutes ago and having her tea for a third time. But then she remembered that the mean-looking man and his friend Harry would soon be coming round to snatch the time machine, and she had to work out a way of stopping them.

She went out into the back yard.

There was a ladder propped up by the back door. Tilly dragged it to the wall behind the shed and climbed up to have a look. The wall was very high and quite difficult to get over, but she wondered if she could make it even more difficult.

She got down off the ladder and went into the shed. Most of the space was filled by the time machine, but there was a cupboard in the corner that was full of the things people usually kept in sheds. Tilly looked inside.

There was a big tub of something called PolyLube that her dad sometimes used on the axles of his bicycle wheels, to make them spin round more easily. It said on the tin that it was 'super slippery'.

Tilly also found the special torch that her dad had once given to her mummy for her birthday. It could shine from both ends, and flash, and turn different colours. Tilly remembered her getting it, because for some reason it had made her mummy cry.

There was also a super-duper megaphone that made your voice sound really loud, and if you pressed a little switch it made a whooping noise like an ambulance. Her dad had made it for school sports day so that he could say things like 'The egg-and-spoon race is about to begin' and everyone would know what was happening. She remembered him setting off the ambulance noise; it was so loud and scary that a lot of children in the reception class had run away.

Then, right at the bottom of the cupboard, she saw a big metal biscuit tin. Tilly knew exactly what was in there. Every Bonfire Night her dad used to make his own fireworks, but those in the biscuit tin were the ones her mummy had asked him not to set off because they were 'too strong'.

'What's "too strong" about them?' her dad had asked her.

'I'll tell you exactly what's "too strong" about them,' she had said. 'Last year they snapped the TV aerial in two and set fire to a tree.'

'But they're a lot safer this year,' he had replied. 'I've only added half the amount of dynamite I used last time.'

But her mummy had still said 'No'.

Tilly opened the tin. The fireworks were packed in very tightly. Some of them looked a bit bent, as if her dad had had trouble squashing them all in, and bits of the powder from inside had spilled out. They looked very dangerous indeed, so Tilly decided to close the lid carefully and put them back where she'd found them.

It was a bit difficult closing the tin: every time she pressed the lid down it popped back up again. In the end she decided it was too dangerous to leave the fireworks so close to the time machine, in case they went off by accident, so she put the lid on as best she could and carried the tin outside. She left it on the garden table, ready to take into the house.

Going back to the cupboard, she also found: an old wire brush, a garden rake, some old tins of paint that were only half full, and something called a rotary clothes line.

The rotary clothes line was used for drying

clothes outside on sunny days. It had
a big pole that went into a hole in the
ground, and on top of that there were five
other poles that stuck out sideways. Between each of
these poles there were three strings of washing line.
It looked a bit like a giant spider's web.

However, her dad, being an inventor, had
'souped it up a bit', as he liked to say. Tilly
remembered asking him what soup had to do with
it, in case there was some delicious soup on offer,
but he told her that 'souping' something up had
nothing to do with soup – souping something up
meant making something more super.

Tilly's dad had fixed the wheel from
the wheelbarrow to the bottom of
the rotary clothes line. He wrapped
a long piece of rope round the
wheel lots and lots and lots of times,
then, as he pulled on the rope, the
whole thing spun round and round at
quite an alarming speed. The harder

he pulled on the rope, the faster it went. 'This'll get the clothes dry in no time,' her dad had said, **pulling** with all his might. But the clothes line had spun round so fast that all the washing had **fallen off!**

Tilly's pyjamas flew off into the lane behind the wall, her dad's shirt ended up in next door's yard, and her mummy's best jumper ended up on the roof!

Tilly remembered her and her dad laughing a lot when it happened, and laughing even more when a pair of knickers flew off and landed on her mummy's head. Her mummy got a bit cross about the whole thing, but unfortunately that just made them laugh even more. Her dad had to go to the shops and bring home a bunch of flowers before her mummy started to see the funny side of things, but after a while she laughed as hard as them.

Tilly smiled to herself at the memory. She liked remembering times when they had all laughed together.

She wondered why her dad didn't like talking about her mummy very much. She knew that he was very sad about her dying, but it seemed as if he wanted to forget about her altogether.

He didn't have any photos of her up on the walls, or on the mantelpiece, or on the dressing table in his bedroom. If Tilly could have had things her own way, she would have filled the whole house with pictures of her mummy.

But she didn't have time to worry about this right now, Tilly told herself; she had to work out what to do.

She had to stop the mean-sounding men from stealing the time machine, otherwise she might never see her dad again. Losing her mummy was bad enough, but losing her dad as well would be a cat's apostrophe. She knew that the real word was *catastrophe*, but her dad always said 'cat's apostrophe' instead of catastrophe because he thought it was a funny joke.

She looked at all the things she'd found in the shed and started to come up with a plan . . .

CHAPTER

An hour and a half later Tilly was sitting fully-dressed by her bedroom window, looking out into the yard. She was waiting for the men to come. She wasn't as scared as she might have been because she had Big Tedder and Mr Fluffybunny propped up on the windowsill to keep her company.

She'd turned off her bedroom light so that no one could see her waiting.

She was just wondering whether there might be time to go downstairs and find a little snack or something when she heard the men in the lane behind the wall. Tilly recognized their voices.

'This is the house, is it?' said the mean-looking one.

'Yeah, he says the machine's in a shed just behind this wall,' said his friend Harry.

'And we just got to smash it up, right?' said the mean-looking man.

'No, no, no! The bloke with the moustache wants it in one piece! If we breaks it, we don't get paid!'

'All right, all right, keep your hair on! Right, give us a leg up and I'll have a quick shufti.'

Tilly heard some grunting – then suddenly a rough pair of hands came up over the wall. But they couldn't get a grip because she had smeared the top of the wall with her dad's 'super-slippery' bicycle stuff!

'Urgh! It's all greasy! I can't grab hold of it!' the mean-looking man said.

'Don't be so stupid! Here – stand on me back and pull yourself up.'

Tilly saw the mean-looking man start to pull himself up on to the wall. She had hoped that the men might give up because they couldn't get over

it, but the mean-looking man was
now sitting on top of the wall, trying to wipe the
super-slippery bicycle stuff off his hands.

'Time for stage two of my plan,' Tilly
whispered to Mr Fluffybunny. She took hold of
the rope and started pulling with all her might.
The rope led out of the window and went all the

way down the yard to the rotary clothes line.
As Tilly pulled on the rope, the clothes line started
to spin.

Tilly had put the clothes line right next to the
wall, and she had tied lots of things on to it: the
wire brush, the rake and the old tins of paint.
She'd put a bit of the super-slippery slippy stuff
around the bottom of the clothes line to make it
spin more easily. The harder she pulled, the faster
it spun round.

The mean-looking man hardly had time to say
'Huh?' before things started hitting him. First he
got the wire brush across his face, then the rake
hit him, then a succession of paint pots bounced
off his bonce. The pots made a noise – *bing,*
bang, bung – which almost made Tilly
laugh out loud. But she didn't have time to laugh
– she had to keep pulling with all her might.

The wire brush scraped across the mean-
looking man's face again, and then the rake
hit him again with a clunk…

and then the paint pots – **bing,**

bang,

bung.

As Tilly pulled harder and harder, the clothes line started spinning faster and faster, and the noises got closer and closer together:

scrape,

clunk,

bing,

bang,

bung,

scrape,
clunk,
bing,
bang,
bung,

scrape-clunk-bing-bang-bung,

scrape-clunk-bing-bang-bung,

scrapeclunkbingbangbung,
scrapeclunkbingbangbung...

'What's happening? Argh! Cor blimey!'
shouted the mean-looking man, waving
his arms about. 'I'm being attacked!'

... scrape clunk bing bang bung ...

... scrape clunk bing bang bung ...

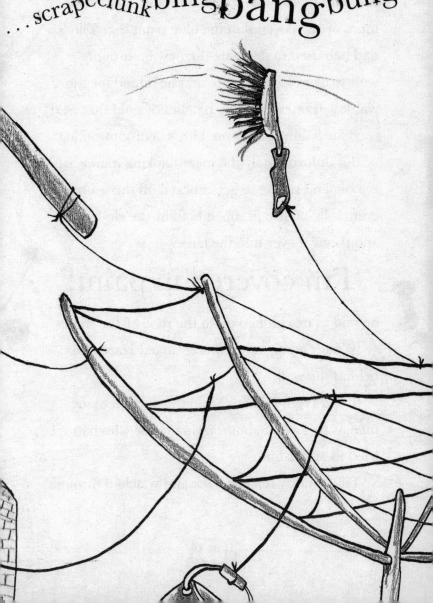

By this time the clothes line was spinning so fast that the paint was coming out of the old tins, and pretty soon the mean-looking man was more or less covered in the blue paint that Tilly's dad had used to decorate the new bathroom, with stripes of gloss white that he'd used for the window frames, and tiny patches of gold that he'd used for painting stars on Tilly's bedroom ceiling.

But unfortunately the mean-looking man was too big and strong to get knocked off the wall, and eventually he just grabbed hold of the clothes line and threw it over into the lane.

'I'm covered in paint!'

he said as he climbed on to the roof of the shed.

'What's going on up there?' asked Harry from behind the wall.

'I don't rightly know,' said the mean-looking man as he looked about, trying to see who had tried to attack him.

Tilly quickly ducked back and watched through

a small gap in the
curtains. The mean-
looking man seemed
to be staring directly
at her window.

'What is it? What's
happening?' asked
Harry.

'Keep your hair on,'
said the mean-looking
man. 'I'm just having a
fag while I assess the situation.'

He fished a packet of cigarettes out of
his pocket and put one in his mouth. Then
he took out a box of matches and struck one.

'Well, what can you see?' said Harry.

'The only thing I can see is a rope leading
up to a toy rabbit and a stuffed bear sitting
on a windowsill,' said the mean-looking man,
lighting his cigarette and tossing the match
into the yard.

Looking through the tiny gap in the curtains, Tilly saw the match land somewhere near the garden table, and it was at just this moment that she realized she'd forgotten to bring the tin of fireworks with the badly fitting lid into the house for safekeeping. She thought she saw a little spark. *Oh no*, she thought. *I hope the lid hasn't popped open again.*

'What? You're being attacked by a toy rabbit and a stuffed bear?' said Harry.

'I dunno. I'm going to investigate,' said the mean-looking man, and he was just about to jump down from the shed roof and walk towards the house when suddenly

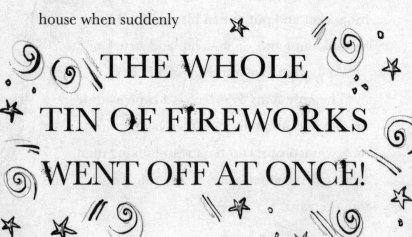

THE WHOLE TIN OF FIREWORKS WENT OFF AT ONCE!

The noise was tremendous!

There were bangs and crunches and cracks and booms. The sky flashed with streaks of orange and red and white and blue, as if a hundred thunderstorms had happened all at once. If Tilly hadn't known what it was, she'd have been very scared indeed.

The mean-looking man looked terrified. By the light of all the fireworks Tilly could see Harry running around in the lane behind the wall. Neither of the men had a clue what was happening.

It was then that she remembered the other part of her plan; the part she had meant to do while the mean-looking man was being hit by the clothes line. She turned on the special torch, choosing the flashing blue light, which reflected off all the windows and walls. If you were a bit stupid, you might have thought a police car had just turned up.

She flipped the switch on the megaphone and the siren noise came on very loudly, just like on school sports day. The mean-looking man looked up in terror.

Then Tilly started speaking into the megaphone. In her best pretend grown-up voice she said:

This is the police! You have been very naughty! We are going to get you and put you in jail.

'Flipping heck, Harry, it's the cops! And they've got shooters! Scarper!' shouted the mean-looking man, jumping back over the wall into the lane.

'Wait for me, Cedric. I can't run as fast as you!' shouted Harry.

Cedric ran off as fast as he could and disappeared round the corner in a flash, while Harry lumbered along after him and eventually, after a lot of huffing and puffing, disappeared round the corner as well.

Tilly switched off the special torch with its flashing blue light and the megaphone with its wailing siren, and for a while she just watched the fireworks. They were beautiful, but she could see her mummy's point – they were rather strong. One of them seemed to go almost all the way to the moon before exploding in a ball of blue and gold sparks. Another one got caught on the telegraph wire behind their house. It spun round and round like a Catherine wheel before going off with an enormous bang and a shower of silver flames.

Very pretty, but very dangerous, Tilly thought as the fireworks started to come to an end.

She was quite pleased with herself. Everything had gone as well as she could have hoped. The men had run off and the time machine was safe.

She was just wondering whether she should give herself another star, and perhaps have another packet of raw jelly as a treat for doing so well, when the very last firework went off.

Tilly watched open-mouthed as it jumped out of the tin and flew straight into the shed! It was some kind of rocket, and she could see it through the shed window as it flew this way and that, **bouncing** off the walls.

It seemed to go on forever. It started getting tangled up in all the wires, then shooting off

again and hitting the computer. It bounced off
the ceiling, and the floor, and the metal booth,
and eventually exploded in a fireball of red and
white sparks. The explosion was so big that Tilly
wondered how the roof of the shed stayed on.

She ran downstairs, out into the yard and down the short path to the shed. She carefully peered round the open door to look inside. The firework had finished, but what she saw made her heart sink. The whole shed was full of black soot and scorch marks, and something was very wrong with the time machine. Some of the lights had stopped twinkling, and it was making a noise like a car engine when it's running out of petrol.

The tangle of wires that had looked like a mass of brightly coloured spaghetti was now like a mess of dirty black shoelaces, and the computer made a funny noise, like a very sad cat miaowing its last miaow. There was a tiny puff of smoke from the keyboard, and then the screen went blank.

The whole machine looked and sounded very ill indeed. It wheezed and gasped, and the lights that were still working got weaker and weaker.

Tilly's bottom lip began to quiver. She wasn't a girl who cried very often, but she couldn't help feeling sorry for herself. If the time machine

106

didn't work, how would she ever see her dad again? She'd lost her mummy, and now she was going to lose her dad as well. It just wasn't fair! And it was all her fault for leaving the tin of fireworks on the garden table!

In a sudden fury she punched the big green button marked GO.

The button *fell off* the machine!

Oh, everything's against me, thought Tilly. She picked up the button, and was just about to throw it out of the door in rage when she heard the machine start making a different noise.

She looked up. Some of the lights seemed to be trying to shine more brightly. A couple of the wheels started spinning slightly, then stopped, then started spinning again. The electric hum pulsed up and down, getting stronger each time. The wires gave off tiny sparks, and bits of the machine that had turned themselves off were now turning themselves back on again.

108

Tilly saw the lights in the little metal booth start to flash. It was as if the machine was asking her to step in.

She cautiously approached the booth and went in. There was a burst of steam, and then she was gone.

CHAPTER

Tilly was very surprised to find herself on the deck of an old-fashioned sailing ship. It had three big masts, and each of the masts had three enormous square sails. It looked like someone had washed a giant's bed sheets and hung them out to dry.

Looking out across the sea, Tilly could see lots of other ships that looked just the same. They were stretched out in a long line, and there must have been about fifty of them. The ship she was on was the first in the line. A little distance away there was another line of about fifty ships, and the two lines were getting closer together.

Lots of men were scurrying about the deck. It looked like they were getting ready for a game of pirates. Tilly had played pirates with her friends at school, but this looked a lot more serious. In fact some of the guns and cannons looked quite real. All in all, it seemed like it was going to be the most realistic game of pirates she had ever seen.

One of the sailors was hurriedly fixing lots of different-coloured flags together.

'Excuse me, but what are you doing?' asked Tilly.

'Well, young midshipman,' said the sailor, 'I'm sending a message to all the British ships from Admiral Nelson. All these different flags mean a different letter or word, see, and if you read them one after the other they spell out a message.'

'Can I help?' said Tilly.

'Of course you can. They're in the right order. You could just fasten them together while I fix the first one to this rope, which goes to the top of the mast.'

Each of the flags had a loop on one end and a toggle on the other, like on the duffel coat Tilly wore that morning. It was quite easy to join them together, and she set to work with gusto.

'What does the message say?' she asked.

'It says, *England expects that every man will do his duty*.'

'What's his duty?'

'Well, his duty is to fight, of course.'

'There's going to be a fight?' asked Tilly, somewhat alarmed. 'A proper fight?'

'Well, of course there is. How can you not know? Where have you been? That's the French Navy we're heading towards!' said the sailor as he hoisted the line of flags up the mast. He would have liked to get a closer look at Tilly, but he was too busy making sure the rope didn't snag.

'You must be one of the youngest midshipmen I've ever seen. In fact I don't recall seeing your face before.'

'Well, you probably haven't,' said Tilly, 'because I only just got here.'

'What? Have you come from another ship?'

'No, I came from the shed at home. I just punched the green button and it fell off, and somehow it made the time machine start working – and poof! Here I was,' said Tilly as she fixed the last flag on to the line.

'What green button?' asked the sailor, hauling away.

'This one,' said Tilly, showing him. 'You can see bits of wire and things hanging out of the back. I think they work the machine.'

'What you talking about? Let's have a look,' said the sailor.

Tilly lifted up the button for him to see, but he was still hauling on the line of flags, and her arms got a bit caught on the rope.

'Keep your hands out of the way!' shouted the sailor, pulling really hard on the rope as the flags shot up the mast.

'But the button!' shouted Tilly. 'My button's got stuck in the flags!'

The big green button had got caught in one of the loops that tied the flags together, and Tilly looked on open-mouthed as the flags and the button were hauled right to the top of the mast!

'ACTION STATIONS! PREPARE TO FIRE!'

came a very loud voice from the other end of the ship. Tilly looked round to see who was doing the shouting, and there were two men in fancy uniforms.

They wore bright blue jackets, white trousers that only came down to the knee, with white tights, and black shoes with gold buckles. Tilly thought their tights and shoes looked like the ones her mummy used to make her wear for 'special occasions'. Each man wore a funny three-cornered hat. It was the kind of hat that looked like a very smart tea cosy, and it was trimmed with gold, with a large silver brooch on the front.

Both men looked very important, although one looked more important than the other. His jacket was decorated with huge medals like stars, and he was wearing a big red sash. Tilly saw that he only had one arm – his right sleeve was empty and was pinned to his chest. And he also had a patch over his right eye.

Tilly walked along the deck towards them. 'Er, excuse me,' she said, tugging on the important-looking man's empty sleeve.

The important-looking man looked down

at her with his good eye. 'Goodness gracious!' he said. 'A young girl! What are you doing here? This is neither the time nor the place for young girls.'

'Oh, we play pirates at school,' said Tilly. 'The girls are really quite good at it – we usually beat the boys.'

'Pirates?' asked the other man, sounding annoyed. 'You think we are pirates?'

'Young lady,' said the important-looking man with one eye, 'we are not pirates. I am Admiral Nelson of His Majesty's Royal Navy, and this is Captain Hardy.'

'Well, you look like pirates,' said Tilly.

'And you think this is a game?' asked Captain Hardy.

'Well, you shouldn't hit people for real,' said Tilly. 'Someone might get hurt. Miss Scarborough says we're not allowed to use sticks when we play pirates in case we have someone's eye out. Is that what happened to you?' She pointed at Admiral Nelson's eye patch.

'GET READY TO FIRE! PREPARE FOR A BROADSIDE ON BOTH THE PORT AND THE STARBOARD SIDES!'

shouted Captain Hardy.

'What's a broadside?' asked Tilly.

'A broadside is when all the cannons on

one side of the ship fire at the same time,' said Admiral Nelson.

'And what's the port side?'

'Well, it's the left-hand side of the ship, while looking forward,' said Admiral Nelson.

'And the starboard?'

'Why, that's the right-hand side of the ship, of course,' he told her, beginning to sound a bit flustered.

Tilly looked round to see that her ship was about to cut through the other line of ships. All the sailors were crouching by their cannons on both the port and starboard sides.

'But this is not the time for idle chatter,' said Admiral Nelson. 'You are the second stranger to appear on deck today. May I ask who you are?'

'I'm Tilly Henderson,' said Tilly. 'And I think I might know who the other stranger was. Did he have messy hair, black glasses with one lens broken, and a slightly burnt beard?'

'That's the very man!'

'Oh, that's my dad,' said Tilly. 'Is he still here?'

'No, he just disappeared. But where have you both come from?'

'Oh, that's easy, we both come from Number 10, Railway Sidings,' said Tilly. 'Do you know it? It's quite near the High Street and very convenient for school.'

'But how did you get here?' said Admiral Nelson, getting even more flustered.

'I don't really know, but I think it's got something to do with that big green button that's stuck up there in those flags,' she said, pointing to the top of the mast. 'Which is why I really need to get it back. Is there any chance we could pull the message down?'

'I'm afraid there's no time – we are about to go into battle,' said Admiral Nelson. 'This day will go down in history as the Battle of Trafalgar.'

'HOLD IT STEADY, LADS!!' shouted Captain Hardy.

Tilly turned to see their ship slide between two of the French ships. She couldn't believe how close they were. She could see the faces of the men on the other ships. They looked quite frightened.

'Quick, you must take cover!' said Admiral Nelson, carefully pushing Tilly into a safe space between two enormous barrels.

'AND FIRE!!!'

screamed Captain Hardy at the top of his voice. All the cannons fired at once, on both sides of the ship. The noise was absolutely incredible, and there was so much smoke that Tilly couldn't see anything for nearly a whole minute.

When the smoke began to clear she saw that their ship had turned alongside one of the French ships, and now the French were firing *their* cannons at *them*!

It was pandemonium. Cannonballs were crashing about, masts were falling down, sails were being ripped apart. Her ship was firing cannonballs at the ship next door, and they were firing back. Sailors were swinging on ropes, trying to get on to each other's ships, and up in the rigging men with old-fashioned guns were shooting at each other and

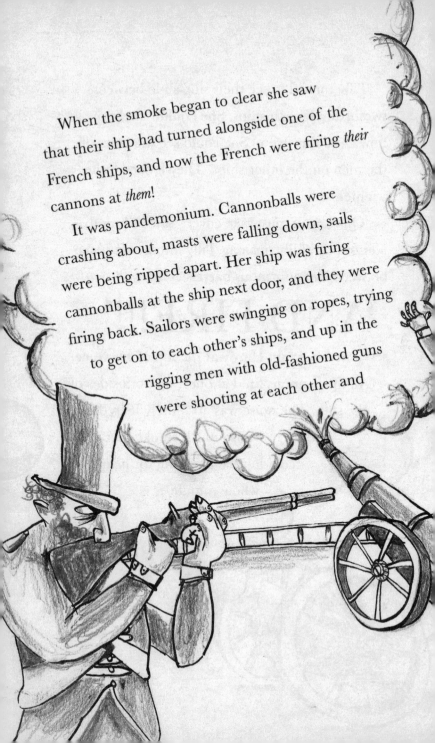

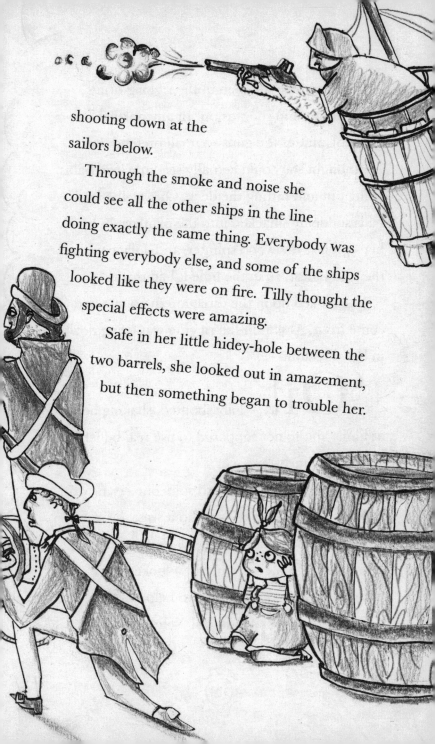

shooting down at the
sailors below.

Through the smoke and noise she
could see all the other ships in the line
doing exactly the same thing. Everybody was
fighting everybody else, and some of the ships
looked like they were on fire. Tilly thought the
special effects were amazing.

Safe in her little hidey-hole between the
two barrels, she looked out in amazement,
but then something began to trouble her.

She could see the men in the rigging firing down at the ship she was on. In any normal game of pirates the guns were all pretend, but she thought she could actually see little lead balls flying out and hitting the deck. One of the lead balls suddenly smacked into the plank right beside her. It made the wood splinter, and Tilly could see the lead ball stuck in the hole it had made.

She looked up in the direction the bullet had come from. A man in the rigging was firing down in her direction.

'**Oi!**' Tilly shouted, shaking her fist at him. 'You're not supposed to use real bullets! You might hurt someone!'

'**I'm hit!**' she heard someone cry nearby.

When she turned to see who it was, she saw Admiral Nelson falling to the deck. Captain Hardy and the men around him looked very alarmed, and they all rushed to help him.

Tilly thought that Admiral Nelson was either

a very good actor or really hurt. He seemed to be in a great deal of pain. With his only arm he signalled for Hardy to come closer, and the captain leaned down to listen to what he wanted to say.

Tilly couldn't quite hear because of all the cannon and gunfire, but she was pretty sure Admiral Nelson said, 'I'd like a KitKat please, Hardy.'

She was immediately relieved – anyone who was asking for a KitKat in the middle of a battle couldn't be properly injured. And the fact that

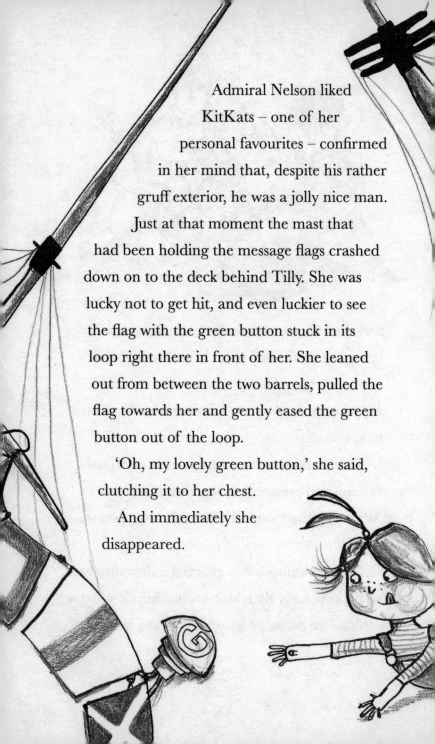

Admiral Nelson liked
KitKats – one of her
personal favourites – confirmed
in her mind that, despite his rather
gruff exterior, he was a jolly nice man.
Just at that moment the mast that
had been holding the message flags crashed
down on to the deck behind Tilly. She was
lucky not to get hit, and even luckier to see
the flag with the green button stuck in its
loop right there in front of her. She leaned
out from between the two barrels, pulled the
flag towards her and gently eased the green
button out of the loop.

'Oh, my lovely green button,' she said,
clutching it to her chest.

And immediately she
disappeared.

CHAPTER

Tilly had never been to a football match before. She'd played football in the playground at school, but she'd never been to a game like the ones shown on TV.

But here she was, right in the middle of an enormous football stadium. It was packed. She didn't have time to count them all, but she thought there must be at least a million people there. And they were all shouting. It was very exciting.

It was a bit like when her dad watched football on the telly, only this was outside, and there were a million people watching instead of just one.

Half of them were waving the Union Jack flag and shouting, 'Come on, England!' The other half were waving a flag that had three stripes – black at the top, red in the middle and yellow at the bottom – and they were shouting something Tilly couldn't quite understand.

She thought they might be from abroad.

On an old-fashioned scoreboard she read:

ENGLAND 2   WEST GERMANY 2

Tilly was standing in one of the goalmouths, and most of the footballers were running around at the other end of the pitch.

She looked at the big green button, which was still in her hand. *I've got to be very careful with this*, she thought to herself. *I mustn't press it unless I really have to, because my dad might be here, and if I go somewhere else I might not be able to find him.*

'*Was machst du hier?*'

Tilly looked round and saw that the goalkeeper was talking to her. She thought he must be one of the German players because he wasn't speaking English, and she remembered her dad saying he'd met a German goalkeeper called Hans something-or-other. He looked rather alarmed to see Tilly standing there.

'*Was machst du hier?*' he said again.

'I'm sorry, I don't understand what you're saying,' said Tilly. 'Are you Hans?'

Luckily the man could speak a bit of English – although he spoke with a very strong German accent – and he said, 'Yes, I am Hans. But what are you here doing, little girl? We in the middle are of a match very important.

This is the World Final Cup!'

'Well, I'm looking for my dad,' said Tilly, who was glad that Hans seemed friendly. 'He invented a time machine, you see, and then he got stuck in time, and then I tried to help him, and then some men tried to steal the machine, and then the machine broke, and then the button came off, and then I nearly cried but I didn't, and then it started working again, and then I was on a pirate ship where I met a man with one eye who likes KitKats, and now I'm here.'

'This is a tale strange. But your father – tall he was, with hair messy, *und* spectacles broken, with beard funny and burnt bits, like someone on fire his face did make?' asked Hans.

'That's him!'

'He earlier was here! He was excited very much to be the match watching. He kept speaking "I cannot believe it is 1966" – fellow strange, what year other could it possible to be? *Und* the most strangely thing was, as I was just with him speaking, he suddenly disappeared! He is where right you are now standing *und* –'

But Hans didn't have time to finish his story because he suddenly noticed that all the footballers were rushing towards his end of the pitch.

'*Schnell!* The *Englisch* this way are coming! The way out of keep! I am not wanting you to become hurt!'

Tilly turned to see one of the English footballers running towards the goal with the ball at his feet.

'Agh!' shouted Hans. 'Not again Geoff Hurst – he is already twice scoring!'

Just at that moment the man
that Hans called Geoff Hurst
gave the ball a hefty boot. It came
very fast and hit the crossbar just
above Tilly. It bounced off the
crossbar straight on to her head
and into the goal. The blow sent
her flying, and as she fell she
knocked the ball out of the goal,
but she could hear all the people with Union
Jacks cheering. She must have scored! That meant
England were winning!

But, as she put her hands out to cushion her
fall, she accidentally pressed the button and
immediately disappeared . . .

CHAPTER

Tilly looked around. She wondered where on earth she was now! Everything looked strangely familiar and unfamiliar at the same time.

She was sitting on the edge of the pavement in a cramped and busy street. Everything was very dirty. It looked like the pictures of Victorian London that Miss Scarborough had put up on the classroom walls.

There were lots of horses pulling carriages and carts. On the pavements women were washing clothes and bed sheets in large tin buckets. Children in rags ran up and down the street; the very smallest were playing with hoops and

spinning tops, but many were carrying bundles,
or selling things, or sweeping the street.

Tilly saw that a lot of the people didn't have
any shoes, and that their clothes were filthy.

The whole place smelled awful. It stank
of horse poo and rotting vegetables, and

Tilly thought something must have gone wrong with the drains – it reminded her of the time when the workmen dug up the sewers at school, and everyone was allowed to go home early.

She was sitting outside a house that looked a lot like her own house at 10 Railway Sidings. In fact the whole street reminded her of Railway Sidings, except there were houses on both sides here.

At the top of the street was a factory that looked just like the one at home, but instead of being closed this factory was full of noise and people and machines, with steam and black smoke billowing out of the big chimneys.

Tilly could smell the smoke; it was blowing through the clothes lines that crisscrossed the street up above her. The clean washing was getting dirty again as soon as it was hung out to dry.

What they need is a rotary clothes line in the back yard, she thought. *What they need is a 'souped-up' rotary clothes line like my dad made, then they could dry the washing in next to no time and take it indoors before it got dirty again.*

But thinking about her dad made her wonder where he was, and that made her a bit sad, so she tried not to think about him.

The whole street was very noisy: the factory was making a roaring sound and people were shouting out, selling pots and pans, or pies, or firewood; and the clatter of the horses' hooves and the metal cartwheels on the cobbled street was deafening.

In fact it was all just a bit too noisy, smelly and confusing for

Tilly, and for the first time since her mummy had died she started to cry.

Her dad didn't really like crying. 'Crying's not going to get us anywhere, is it? Best put on a brave face and get on with it,' he usually said.

Tilly thought he was probably right, but sometimes she just wanted a really good cry, and right now that's exactly what she did. She hadn't had a proper cry for so long, and once she got started she really let go. She had a real 'boohoo' of a cry, and before long her face was wet with salty tears and her nose was running.

'What you crying so hard about?' came a voice.

Tilly looked round. It was a boy about her own age. He was dressed in filthy ragged clothes and had no shoes. Any bits of his body that showed were covered in coal dust and soot. But he had a kind face.

'I never seen anyone cry so hard. If you cries any harder you'll likely start a river right here in the street!' he said with a cheeky grin.

Tilly could see that he was trying to cheer her up. She looked at him and he smiled broadly and put his hand on her shoulder to comfort her.

'My name's Jack. Can I help at all?' he asked.

His kindness made the world seem a better place, and slowly but surely Tilly stopped crying. Once she'd stopped completely she wiped her face on her sleeve.

'My best friend at school is called Jack,' she said.

'You go to school, do you? Cor, you're lucky. I never been to school. I'd love to learn reading and writing. Here, what's your name?'

'My name's Tilly. Could you tell me where we are?' she asked.

'Well, this here street's Back Lane, but they say as they'll change all the street names round here once they've done building the railway sidings next door.'

'No, I mean, in time,' said Tilly.

'Why, it's knocking on six o'clock in the evening – leastways that's what it says on that clock over there,' he said, pointing at the clock on the church tower nearby. Tilly thought the church and the clock seemed familiar. It looked like the church on the High Street near her house, but the clock on this one was working.

'No, I mean, what year?' asked Tilly.

'Blimey, no church clock's going to tell you what year it is. I'm not sure as I know myself. I can only tell you that it's the queen's golden jubilee this year.'

'Queen Elizabeth?' asked Tilly.

'Queen Elizabeth? Who's she? No, I mean *our*

queen, our *British* queen – Queen Victoria.'

The penny dropped, and Tilly realized that she was actually back in Victorian times. She looked around at the busy street, with all the horses and people scurrying about. *Oh, Miss Scarborough would love this*, she thought to herself. *Though she'd probably tell us all to get our worksheets out and start drawing pictures of everything!*

'Where do you live?' asked Jack.

'I live at 10 Railway Sidings,' said Tilly.

'Well, I never heard of that street, but I live here, at 10 Back Lane,' he said, pointing at the red door behind them. 'You're very welcome to come in for a nice cup of tea, if you like.'

'Oh, yes please,' said Tilly, hoping there might be something like an iced bun to go with it.

'Here! What you doing home so early?' came a loud, gruff voice.

They both turned to see an enormous man with a face like an angry bulldog striding towards them. He grabbed Jack by the scruff of the neck

and pulled him up off the ground with one hand.
Jack's legs were left dangling in the air.

'I told you not to leave the duke's house until you'd finished sweeping all them chimneys!' shouted the man.

'But, Mr Wormwood, sir, we did them. We swept them all, sir. I promise you. All of them, sir – clean as a whistle.'

Mr Wormwood snarled and studied Jack's face carefully, trying to work out if he was telling the truth or not. 'If I finds out you're lying, I'll stick you down a chimney that's got a fire lit down below, you understand?'

Although Tilly was afraid for Jack, she couldn't help staring at Mr Wormwood's arm – the one hanging down by his side: on his wrist was a watch. It looked exactly like the one her mummy had given to her dad! She could even hear it ticking. It sounded exactly the same too!

'If you lets me down, all them posh people will stop asking me to clean their chimneys, and I likes doing all them posh people's houses because they pays top whack. In fact I've got a very tasty job for you tomorrow,' Mr Wormwood told Jack.

'I'm telling the truth, Mr Wormwood, sir, honest I am,' said Jack.

'All right then,' said Mr Wormwood, letting him drop to the ground. Then he suddenly swung round to stare straight into Tilly's face. 'What you gawping at?'

Tilly shrank back in fright.

'Hey! I said, what you gawping at?' he shouted, breathing stinky breath into her face. His teeth were mostly yellow and green, and some were black.

I bet he doesn't get any gold stars for cleaning his teeth, thought Tilly.

'I'm sorry, Mr Wormwood, I was looking at your watch.'

Mr Wormwood's attitude suddenly changed. He straightened up, his frown melted away and a thin smile creased the corners of his mouth. He seemed very pleased that Tilly had noticed

his watch. 'Oh yeah,' he said. 'It's one of them new-fangled arm watches. Nice piece, ain't it?'

'Arm watch?' asked Tilly.

'Oh yeah, it's called an arm watch because you wears it on your arm. It's the very latest thing. I acquired it this very morning. The old pocket watch is on its way out. This is the modern way. You tells the time just by raising your arm.'

Mr Wormwood was absolutely delighted with his watch, and very happy to show off about it.

He let his arm hang down by his side, and then raised it quickly to look at his watch, just to show how easy it was.

'Much easier than fumbling for the old pocket watch,' he said, and then he mimed fumbling for an old pocket watch in his waistcoat pockets. He took a long time over it, pretending to look in one pocket and then the other, and then pretending to have great difficulty getting it out.

'You see?' he said. 'An unnecessary palaver. Whereas . . .' And he quickly raised his wrist again to show how much quicker the new watch was. 'Easy as pie!'

Tilly didn't know what to do. She wanted to get a closer look to see if it actually was her dad's watch, but she didn't want to make Mr Wormwood angry because she'd seen what he'd done to Jack.

'The best thing about that watch is that it can tell you the day and the date, and what time sunrise and sunset are going to be,' she said.

Mr Wormwood looked puzzled. He looked at the watch, and then he looked at Tilly. 'How's it do that then?' he said.

Tilly stood up and moved towards him. He was truly ginormous and towered above her. But, being as brave as she could, she reached up and pointed at the face of the watch.

'You see, this dial here tells you the day of the week, this one tells you the date, this one tells you the month, and these two rings say what time sunrise and sunset are going to be.'

Mr Wormwood looked confused and very interested at the same time. 'How do you know about these things?' he asked.

'Because my dad's got one. In fact I can tell you that your watch is set wrong – it says the sun should have set already, but you can see it hasn't.' Tilly pointed at the sun, which she could just make out through the smoke and smog.

Mr Wormwood looked at the watch, and then looked at the sun shining weakly through the polluted air. Then he examined the watch more closely. He could see that Tilly was right.

'If you like, I could set it to the right day and date,' said Tilly. 'My dad showed me how to do it.'

Mr Wormwood stared at her suspiciously. Then he looked at the sun again and back to the watch. He suddenly thrust his arm out towards her and said, 'Go on then.'

'No, you'll have to take it off,' said Tilly. 'I can't get to the controls if it's on your wrist.'

He didn't really want to take the watch off, but he could see that if he wanted it to work properly he had to, so he slowly undid the strap and held it out to her.

Tilly took it and straight away turned it over to look at the back – and there was the engraving!

TO MY DARLING JOHN,

I WILL LOVE YOU FOR ALL TIME,

LOVE JULIA X

'This is my dad's watch!' she shouted.

'What you talking about?' said Mr Wormwood,

grabbing at the watch, but Tilly held on to it.

'This is my dad's watch!'

she said again. 'I can prove it because it's got the writing on the back. John is my dad, and Julia is my mummy!'

'It's *my* watch!' shouted Mr Wormwood, grabbing Tilly by the scruff of the neck and lifting her up in the air, just like he had Jack. 'I'll admit that it may have had a previous owner, but I got it fairly. I'm a hard man, but I'm no thief! Hard but fair.'

He plucked the watch out of Tilly's hands and dropped her on the ground. Tilly fell in a heap.

'How did you get it then?' she asked, almost bursting into tears again. 'It's my dad's watch. How did you get it if you didn't steal it from him?'

'Well, I'll tell you, young lady,' said Mr Wormwood, leaning right over her. 'I swapped it. This morning I had the good fortune to find a most peculiar shiny green mushroom in the street. This man saw that I had it, and said he'd swap me his arm watch for it. Well, being as the mushroom was no good to eat, I agreed.'

Tilly felt in her pockets for the big green button marked GO – it had gone! When had she lost it? She didn't know. Maybe she and the button had arrived at different times.

'This shiny green mushroom,' said Tilly. 'Do you mean it was plastic? And did it have the word "go" written on it?'

'What's "plastic"? I never heard that word before. It did have some letters on it, it's true. But I don't know what they were cos I can't read – cos I never had no schooling.'

'And the man you swapped it with – did he have wild curly hair, and glasses with one of the lenses broken, and a beard that looked a bit burnt?'

'That's the man!' said Mr Wormwood. 'And he spoke in riddles. Said something about – oh, it was mad talk – something about worms in holes. I think he might have escaped from the lunatic asylum cos he was jabbering on about meeting the queen.'

'That's my dad,' said Tilly, looking at Jack. 'I know it – that's my dad.'

'Our Jack here's got more chance of meeting the queen,' said Mr Wormwood, turning to Jack. 'Cos tomorrow, Jackie boy, your job is to clean the chimneys at Buckingham Palace! You got that? Buckingham Palace, where the queen lives. I wants you and the rest of the lads round there, Buckingham Palace, back gate, at six in the morning sharp. You got that?'

'Buckingham Palace. Back gate. Six o'clock sharp. Yes, Mr Wormwood, sir,' said Jack.

And, with that, Mr Wormwood grunted at

Jack, then grunted at Tilly and strode off down the street.

'I bet you're ready for that cup of tea now, ain't you?' said Jack.

Tilly really wanted a cup of tea, and perhaps a chocolate eclair or a slice of lemon drizzle cake, but she was worried about losing the green button. It sounded like her dad had it, but she didn't know where he was. 'I think I'd better look for my dad,' she said. 'It's hard to explain, but if I don't find him I think I might be stuck here forever.'

'Well, London's a mighty big city,' said Jack. 'You could walk up and down every street for a year and never see the same one twice.'

'But I've got to find him!' she said, beginning to panic.

'Well, I tell you what – why don't you have a cup of tea first and a bite to eat? You can't start looking on an empty stomach.' Jack smiled at Tilly, and she was so pleased to have a friend that she agreed.

'All right,' she said. 'Thank you very much.'

'Come on – let me introduce you to the rest of
my family,' said Jack, leading her into the house.

His family was very big. He had ten brothers
and sisters! They were all very kind to her and,
when they found out that she had no brothers and
sisters at all, they went out of their way to make
her feel welcome.

Jack's house was almost exactly the same as Tilly's, except it didn't have a new bathroom in the back yard. In fact it didn't have a bathroom at all. If Jack's family wanted water they had to use the pump outside, and if they wanted the loo they had to go to the public toilet at the top of the street.

There were no iced buns for tea, no chocolate

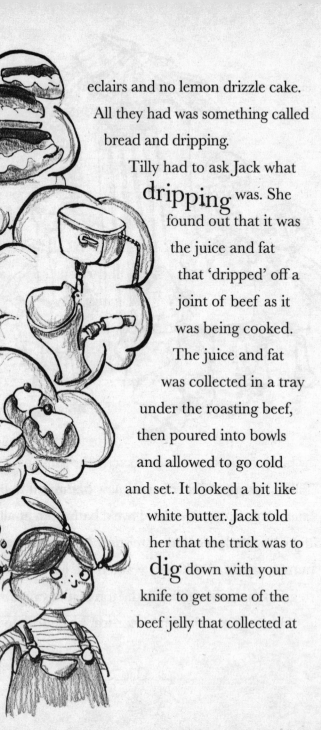

eclairs and no lemon drizzle cake.
All they had was something called
bread and dripping.

Tilly had to ask Jack what
dripping was. She
found out that it was
the juice and fat
that 'dripped' off a
joint of beef as it
was being cooked.
The juice and fat
was collected in a tray
under the roasting beef,
then poured into bowls
and allowed to go cold
and set. It looked a bit like
white butter. Jack told
her that the trick was to
dig down with your
knife to get some of the
beef jelly that collected at

the bottom of the bowl. Then you spread the jelly and the white buttery fat on a slice of bread and ate it.

Tilly was a bit unsure at first, but she was always brave about trying new foods so she took a little bite and . . . it was delicious! The beef jelly was like the best bit of gravy at the bottom of the pan. She'd never tasted anything so beefy! She polished off two big hunks of bread slathered with dripping in double-quick time, and that pretty much filled her up.

When she asked Jack what they did with the roast beef, he told her that they couldn't afford the actual beef. He told her that rich families bought the beef, and that families like his just bought the dripping.

Tilly always had her best ideas when she'd had something to eat, and once she'd eaten her bread and dripping and drunk two cups of tea her brain started working again.

'Mr Wormwood said my dad was jabbering on about going to see the queen, didn't he?' she said to Jack. 'And you're going to Buckingham Palace to sweep the chimneys tomorrow, aren't you?'

'That's right,' said Jack.

'Well, if I could come with you, I could get into the palace and maybe, if my dad is there, I could find him,' said Tilly.

'That's a brilliant idea!' said Jack. 'But if you're going to come with me tomorrow we'd better get to bed – we've got to be up at five.'

Tilly was a bit surprised to find that Jack shared a bed with his brothers and sisters, except for the two smallest ones who slept with Jack's parents in the next room. It still meant that there were nine of them in the bed – ten with Tilly – and even sleeping top to tail there wasn't much room. Tilly lay there and looked up. There was a little dent in the ceiling that looked exactly like the dent in her ceiling at home.

She tried to work out what it all meant, but she was so tired from all her adventures that she soon fell asleep.

CHAPTER

At six o'clock the next morning Tilly and Jack
– along with seven other boys – were waiting
outside Buckingham Palace. They were all very
grimy and dirty, even Tilly!

Jack said that if she was going to pretend to
be a chimney sweep, she'd have to look like one,
otherwise Mr Wormwood would recognize her for
sure. So after breakfast he'd given her a cap and
taken her out to the back yard and covered her
from head to foot in ashes and soot from the ash
bucket. By the time he'd finished Tilly looked like
she hadn't had a bath in years.

'Who's that?' came the gruff voice of Mr

Wormwood as he approached the gang of chimney sweeps outside the palace. He was pointing straight at Tilly.

Tilly's knees started to shake.

'It's my little brother Billy, Mr Wormwood, sir. Begging your pardon, he'd like to learn the trade, so I brought him along,' said Jack.

Mr Wormwood looked at Tilly carefully.

'Billy, eh? He looks familiar,' he said.

'Well, he is my brother, sir,' said Jack. 'There must be a family likeness.'

'There's no telling whether he'll be any good as a sweep, so I can't pay him more than a penny for the day's work, you understand?'

'Yes, sir, Mr Wormwood, sir. I'll keep an eye on him, sir, don't you worry. And I'll teach him good,' said Jack.

Mr Wormwood told the policeman at the gate what their business was, and all the young sweeps filed into the palace with their brushes and poles and set to work.

Tilly learned that being a sweep was very hard work indeed. They went from room to room in the big palace. In each room they covered the fireplace with an enormous sheet, then they pushed the circular broom head up the chimney, adding on pole after

162

pole to make the broom
longer, until it popped out
at the top. After the first
sweeping, one of the boys would
climb up the inside of the chimney
with a small brush and sweep out all
the nooks and crannies that the circular
broom couldn't reach.

It was very dirty work, and
Tilly could hear the boys
coughing and wheezing as
the soot filled their lungs.
The good thing was that, as they
went from chimney to chimney, Tilly
could explore each room for any sign
of her dad. But she couldn't find
anything.

At lunchtime they stopped for
twenty minutes, and Jack got out
some bread and cheese that he'd
wrapped in a hanky and put in his

pocket. The bread was black with soot, but Tilly ate it anyway because she was really hungry.

After the short lunch break they got straight back to sweeping. Tilly couldn't believe how hard Jack and his friends worked. She tried to help, but Jack said she'd only get in the way. He said he would do all the work while she kept an eye out for clues.

Unfortunately there didn't seem to be any clues. In fact Tilly didn't really know what a clue would look like, unless her dad was actually standing there.

Towards the middle of the afternoon Jack was just preparing the next chimney when Mr Wormwood strode into the room.

'How's the new lad doing?' he asked, looking at Tilly. 'Why, he don't look like he's done no work at all!'

'I was just showing him how we sets up the sheet,' said Jack. 'And how we puts the broom up and adds on the poles.'

'That's no good!'

screamed Mr Wormwood. 'He's not going to learn nothing from all that! He wants to get straight up a chimney and see what it's all about.

Come on, lad,' he said to Tilly. 'Let's get you up this one and see what you're made of.'

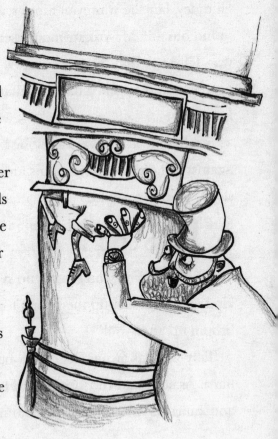

He pulled her roughly towards the big fireplace and pushed her inside. Tilly looked up the chimney. It was dark and dirty, and really quite frightening.

'Come on – up you go!' said Mr Wormwood, shoving her into the darkness. 'Now, spread your elbows and knees, push yourself against the sides, and up!'

Tilly was scared. She was scared of the chimney, but she was even more scared of being found out – if Mr Wormwood discovered that she was Tilly, not Billy, he might throw her out of the palace, and then she'd have no chance of finding her dad.

So she did as she was told. She braced herself against the walls with her arms and legs, and slowly started to climb.

'Faster!' shouted Mr Wormwood. 'You won't make no sweep at that kind of speed. Get up there, or I'll push the broom up after you!'

Tilly went as fast as she could, but it was very hard. As she climbed, she scraped her elbows and knees on the sides of the chimney. Wherever she put her hands soot flew off, and she couldn't help but breathe it in, which made her cough and splutter.

'Not fast enough!' shouted Mr Wormwood, down below. 'Here comes the broom!'

Tilly looked down and saw the big circular broom being pushed up the chimney beneath her. She could hear Mr Wormwood attaching an extra pole, and the next thing she knew it was banging against her feet.

'Come on! Up you go! Or I'll sweep you off the sides and let you fall!' shouted Mr Wormwood.

Tilly had no choice but to climb faster. She climbed further and further, and the chimney got darker and darker. After a while it was so dark she couldn't see anything at all. She could just feel the broom banging against her legs, and hear Mr Wormwood shouting at her from below.

The chimney wasn't straight. She could feel it turning first to the right and then to the left, and then when she looked up she saw a small circle of light above her. *That must be the top of the chimney*, she realized. The thought that she might get out soon cheered her up, and she started climbing even faster.

The higher she got, the narrower the chimney became.

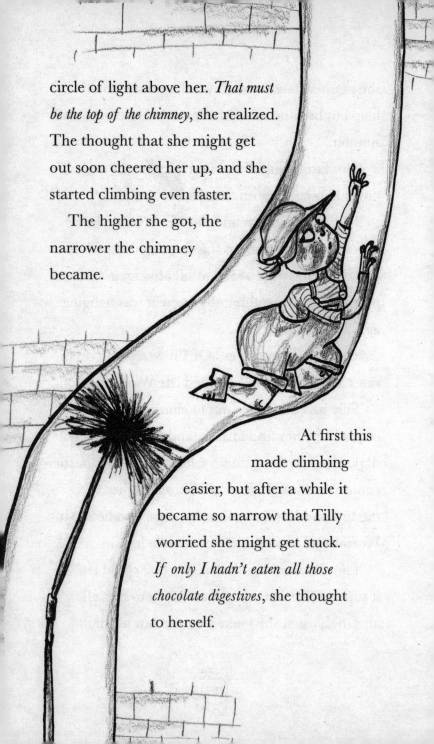

At first this made climbing easier, but after a while it became so narrow that Tilly worried she might get stuck. *If only I hadn't eaten all those chocolate digestives*, she thought to herself.

But the broom was still pushing up beneath her, and this helped her through. With a big effort she clambered up and up, and suddenly found herself poking out of the chimney.

She climbed out on to the roof.

She had never been so dirty! Every time she moved, clouds of soot fell off her clothes.

The roof was very high, and looking around Tilly could see all of London spread out before her. The tallest buildings were the church spires, and there were hundreds of them in every direction. There was one quite close by that stood out from all the rest. It twinkled in the sun and looked like it was made of gold.

The roof of the palace was flat, and Tilly had a good old explore, peering down into the yards, the parade ground and the gardens below. She was looking for any sign of her dad, but she still couldn't see anything.

After a while she thought she'd better go back down, otherwise Mr Wormwood would get cross

with her, but she couldn't remember which
chimney she'd come up! There were trails of
soot in every direction, and all the chimney pots
looked exactly the same.

She began walking backwards, trying to
remember each step she'd taken, and ended up
at a chimney that seemed familiar.

This is the one, she told herself, and she
clambered in and started to inch her way down.

Any minute now it'll turn to the right, thought
Tilly, but when she got to the first bend it went
left.

That's odd – perhaps I
just remembered it wrong. Or
perhaps it's the wrong chimney, and
I ought to go back and try anoth–
But, before she had a chance to
think anything else, she lost her grip on
the walls of the chimney and started
to fall. Down and down she fell,
banging off the walls, causing great
clouds of soot to cascade after her.
She scraped her knees and
elbows and hit her head, and
finally landed in a heap in
the middle of a grand
fireplace.

She was too shocked
and hurt to do
anything other than
just lie there. She had
disturbed so much
soot on the way down

that the room was filled with a giant black cloud. She thought she could hear someone coughing and, as the soot slowly cleared, she became aware of someone in the room looking at her.

The person looking at her was quite old, quite short and quite wide, and she was dressed entirely in black. Her hair was grey and tied up in a bun, and she had something that looked like a white lace hanky pinned on top of her head. Tilly thought she looked just like the picture of Queen Victoria she'd seen in her school book.

'Goodness gracious,' said the old lady. 'Are you all right, little boy?'

'I'm not a boy, I'm a girl,' said Tilly.

'A girl? What's a girl doing up my chimney?' said the old lady, picking up a little handbell and ringing it.

'I'm looking for my dad,' said Tilly.

'Is your papa the chimney sweep?' asked the old lady as two servants dressed in smart uniforms rushed in. The servants saw what

had happened and came to lift Tilly out of the
fireplace.

'No, he's an inventor,' said Tilly.

The servants took hold of her arms and legs.

'Be gentle with her,' said the old lady. 'She's
only a little girl.'

'I'm not that little,' said Tilly as the two servants lifted her up. 'I'm actually average height for my age.'

'Lucky you,' said the old lady. 'I'm actually below average height for my age.'

Something about this made Tilly laugh.

The old lady must have been quite important because when Tilly laughed the two servants seemed quite alarmed. They looked at the old lady to see if Tilly's laughing was going to make her cross. But she wasn't cross. In fact Tilly's laughing made her laugh.

And the old lady laughing made Tilly laugh even more. And, in turn, Tilly's laughing made the old lady laugh even more. And finally even the servants were laughing, although they didn't know exactly what they were laughing at.

As the laughter eventually died down, Tilly looked around the room. It was a very posh room with lots of beautiful furniture and ornaments, and a thick layer of soot was settling over it all.

'I'm sorry about the mess,' she said. 'I didn't mean to make it, I promise.'

'Oh, it's not a complete cat's apostrophe,' said the old lady. 'I've got lots of servants – it'll give them something to do.'

'That's weird,' said Tilly. 'You say "cat's apostrophe" too! The only other person I've ever heard say it is my dad.'

The old lady looked at her with a quizzical eye. 'I only heard it myself for the first time this morning,' she said. 'Your papa – your "dad", as you say – does he have wild hair, broken spectacles and a burnt beard?'

'Yes! Yes, he does! That's my dad! Have you seen him?'

'He was here this very morning,' said the old lady. 'He told me he had travelled through time. And to prove it he showed me a brand-new invention from the future that he called the "mobile phone" – it could make photographic images; it could make telephonic calls without a

wire; it could tell the time, perform tunes like a
musical box and even let you play a game called
Angry Birds. It was a most ingenious device.'

'Do you know where he is now?' asked Tilly.
'It's important that I find him.'

'I'm afraid he simply disappeared,' said the old
lady. 'One minute he was standing right in front
of me, and the next – poof! – he was gone.'

'Oh no,' said Tilly. 'At this rate I'll never find him.' And her bottom lip began to quiver.

The old lady came over and examined Tilly more closely. 'Have you also travelled through time?' she asked.

'Yes,' said Tilly. 'I was only trying to go back to my sixth birthday when my mummy was still alive, but somehow things got a bit out of control.'

The queen nodded as if she understood, then she said to the servants: 'Take this young girl of average height for her age and tend to her wounds. Give her a good wash, dress her in some fresh clothes and then bring her to my sitting room for afternoon tea.'

And with that she swept out of the room.

CHAPTER

Tilly was whisked off to another part of the palace, and seven maids in crisp uniforms suddenly appeared and set to work on her.

When Tilly asked who the old lady was, the maids laughed. 'Why, that's Queen Victoria, you silly little fool,' they said.

'I don't believe it!' said Tilly. 'I've actually met Queen Victoria, just like Dad said!' Then, after a little thought, she said, 'I may be a fool, but I'm not a little one. I'm actually an average-sized fool for my age.'

This made the maids laugh again. They took to Tilly at once and decided to make her look as nice as they possibly could.

They bathed her and scrubbed her and washed her and buffed her, until she was the cleanest she had ever been.

They tended to her cuts and grazes with ointments and bandages.

They curled her hair into ringlets and tied it up with a satin bow.

They rouged her cheeks and powdered her face.

And they dressed her in petticoats and long white socks and a big puffed-out dress with big puffed-out sleeves all trimmed in lace, and black satin slippers, and a broad silk sash that matched the ribbon in her hair.

When Tilly looked in the mirror she didn't recognize herself. 'Who's that?' she said, and all the maids burst out laughing again. 'I look like an enormous frilly mushroom!' she said, and they laughed even more.

*

When Tilly was delivered to the sitting room, Queen Victoria was there, waiting for her. They sat on fancy chairs with a small table in front of them, and on the table was a sight that made Tilly beam with joy. It was a real Victorian afternoon tea!

It looked just like the picture Tilly had drawn at school: there were finger sandwiches, and fruit tarts, and miniature cakes, and macaroons, and freshly baked scones with little pots of cream and strawberry jam. All served on a three-tiered cake stand.

'Oh, this is just the best!' squealed Tilly. 'This is exactly like the picture I drew for my project on the Victorians at school!'

The queen chuckled. 'So, I'm studied at school in the future, am I? Well, do tuck in!'

Tilly reached forward, and on her very best behaviour – because she was in the presence of royalty – she carefully lifted a brightly coloured macaroon from the middle plate and took a

bite. Her mummy had told her that posh people only took very small bites, so she politely took the teeny-tiniest nibble of the macaroon. It was absolutely **scrummy**.

But what happened next took Tilly completely by surprise: the queen reached forward and, in a flurry of hands and teeth and lips, **scoffed** her way through everything on her side of the cake stand in double-quick time!

Finger sandwiches went in whole, miniature cakes went in two at a time, the macaroons flew, and the scones with cream and jam looked like a blur of red and white.

Tilly had only managed to eat a single macaroon in the time it took the queen to finish everything on her side. It was just as Jack, her friend from school, had discovered when he was doing his project on the queen. And when she had finished she rang a little bell and a servant came in and took hold of the cake stand, ready to take it away.

'Excuse me,' said Tilly, feeling rather miffed, 'but I haven't finished! I've only had one macaroon!'

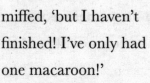

The servant didn't know what to do and looked at the queen. The queen seemed surprised.

This didn't normally happen. Usually, when she had finished eating, everything was cleared away and no one made a fuss.

Tilly reached forward and slowly peeled the servant's hand off the three-tiered stand.

'Right,' she said. 'I think I'll have a scone with cream and jam now.' And she took a small knife and started spreading cream and jam on top of a scone.

The queen's expression slowly changed from one of shock to a smile, and she waved the servant away.

'This is a really lovely afternoon tea,' said Tilly. 'But I think I know one thing that would make it even better.'

'What's that?' asked the queen.

'Party sausages on sticks.'

'Party sausages on sticks?' The queen sounded rather confused.

Tilly explained what they were, and the queen said, 'I think that is a most excellent idea – one can never have enough meat, and from now on I shall always have party sausages with my afternoon tea!'

Tilly nodded her approval and set to work on a couple of finger sandwiches, though she carefully set the smoked-salmon sandwich to one side.

The queen watched her eat, and smiled. 'You know,' she said, 'when you made me laugh this afternoon, it was the first time I'd laughed since my dear husband, Albert, died.'

'Oh dear – did he die quite recently?' asked Tilly.

'No, he died twenty-six years ago.'

'And you're still wearing black funeral clothes?' Tilly was rather surprised.

'Yes, because I miss him so very much. I still think about him all the time.'

'When my mummy died I wore my most colourful pretty dress. My dad wore black, but he only wore it for the day of the funeral. After that he forgot about my mummy altogether.'

The queen thought about this for a moment, then she said, 'Perhaps he still misses her but finds remembering her makes him too sad.' And then she added, 'And perhaps I have shared my sadness about Albert for too long.'

'Was he a nice man?' asked Tilly.

'Oh, he was lovely,' said the queen.

'So was my mummy,' said Tilly as she helped herself to another fruit tart.

'Do you know, I built a huge memorial in his honour. It takes up a whole acre of land, it's taller than a lot of churches and it's covered in real gold,' said the queen. Then, after a little pause, she added, 'I think I might have gone a bit over the top.'

'Yes, I think you have,' said Tilly, reaching for a miniature sponge cake. 'I'd just like a picture of Mummy in every room so that I can always see her. We've only got five rooms, so it would only be five photos. But I don't think my dad would like it.'

The queen watched Tilly polish off the last scone, and sighed. 'Tilly,' she said, 'I've really enjoyed meeting you, and I would like to keep you with me forever, but I think your papa – your "dad" – will be missing you. I think you should go back to your own time.'

'But I don't know how to,' said Tilly.

'I may be able to help you,' said the queen as she moved to a small desk and opened one of the drawers. Tilly could hardly believe her eyes when the queen pulled out the big green button marked GO.

'The button!' she cried.

'When your father vanished, this suddenly appeared where he had been standing,' said the queen. 'I don't know how it works, but I imagine you do?'

'All I know is that when I press it I go somewhere else,' said Tilly.

The queen handed her the button, and she gave the queen a big hug.

'You actually are quite small, aren't you?' said
Tilly.

The queen smiled. 'Go on, be off with you.'

And Tilly pressed
the button . . .

CHAPTER

Tilly found herself all alone in a very serious-looking office. All the furniture was dark brown: the desk, the chair, the filing cabinets – even the carpet. And everything was extremely neat and tidy. All the pencils were lined up in a row. Two boxes labelled POST IN and POST OUT were positioned very carefully at the corners of the desk. And the framed photographs looked like a line of soldiers on parade.

Tilly peered at the photos. In quite a few of them she could see the man with the moustache! It was definitely him. There was a photo of him making a speech in front of lots of men in suits;

and another of him looking very pleased with himself, standing outside Number 10, Downing Street.

Tilly knew that Number 10, Downing Street, was an important place where someone important lived, but whenever someone on *The News* mentioned it her dad would always say, 'Yes, but it's not as important as Number 10, Railway Sidings, is it, Tilly? No, because that's where *we* live!'

Tilly was sitting on the chair behind the desk. There was a computer right in front of her. Someone had been writing a letter on it. Tilly couldn't help reading it because she had noticed her dad's name, John Henderson.

This is what the letter said:

```
Dear Sir,
It is my opinion that John
Henderson will never invent a time
machine. He is simply wasting time
and money. I suggest we let him go
as soon as possible.
Yours faithfully,
Sir Digby Snottington
```

Tilly started to piece things together. She must be in the Government Research Centre! And this was obviously the letter that had made her dad lose his job! She could see an envelope addressed to the Minister for Science and Technology lying on the desk beside her, ready for the letter.

Tilly had a little think, then she carefully put down the green button with GO on it on the desk and started to change the letter. It took her some time because she had to move the cursor about, and erase some words, and put others in their place. After she had finished, the letter looked like this:

```
Dear Sir,
It is my opinion that I will
never invent anything. I am
simply a waste of time and money.
I suggest you let me go as soon
as possible.
Yours faithfully,
Sir Digby Snottington
PS You smell of poo.
PPS Dog poo.
```

Tilly pressed PRINT, and the printer burst into life and printed out the letter. Then she folded it as carefully as possible, put it in the envelope and put the envelope in the POST OUT box.

She looked around. It was time to find her dad if she could. She was pretty sure he had been to the research centre in the time machine because he had reprogrammed the robot dog.

Tilly went over to the door, opened it a fraction and peeked out.

She saw an enormous, brightly lit room full of scientists in white coats. Tilly wondered if this was what her dad meant by a 'laboratory'. There were lots of different workbenches and drawing boards, and all the scientists were busy talking in two and threes. They were pointing at plans and arguing with each other, and tinkering with bits of equipment. It was really quite noisy, much noisier than school. Miss Scarborough would have told them all to be quiet and think about their behaviour.

This is where my dad used to work, thought Tilly. He had often told her about this room, and the

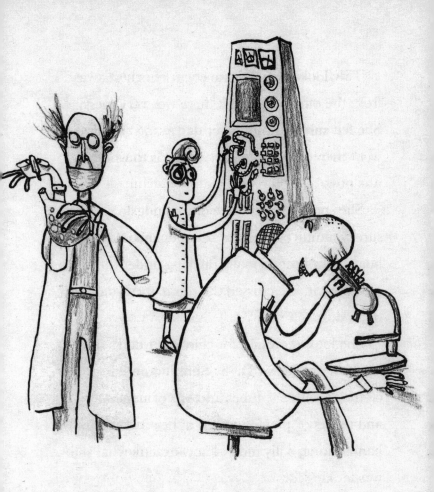

noise that made it hard to think, and how he used
to work at the desk in the corner, as far away
from Sir Digby Snottington's office as possible.
Although her dad used to call him Sir Digby
Snotface.

Tilly looked over at the corner furthest away from the office. The desk there was very messy. She felt sure it must be her dad's, and that if she went there, she might find a clue as to where he was now.

She sneaked out of the office and, slowly but surely, hiding behind the benches and drawing boards, and occasionally ducking under the desks as she went, she crossed the room and found her dad's desk.

She looked around for clues. Her dad's desk wasn't a bit like Sir Digby Snottington's. It was cluttered with test tubes and bits of machinery, and pieces of paper covered in her dad's scribbly handwriting. Tilly didn't know exactly what she was looking for.

To one side of the desk there was a cupboard, and on the cupboard door was a sign that said DO NOT OPEN. Tilly knew that if a grown-up told you not to do something you shouldn't do it, but after thinking very hard for nearly two seconds she decided she had to open it in case there was an important clue inside. She slowly opened the cupboard door . . . and suddenly she saw lots of pictures of her mummy!

They were all taped to the back of the door: there were pictures of her and Tilly's dad when they first met, and pictures of her at their wedding, and pictures of her with Tilly when Tilly was a little baby, and pictures of them all

My darling Julia

on holiday together. In every picture her mummy was smiling, and across the top of the door her dad had scribbled in felt pen: *My darling Julia.*

'MY DARLING JULIA!'

Tilly suddenly shouted out loud. 'That's the password! Mydar lingju lia is the same thing but with the spaces in different places!' She couldn't believe that her dad was using her mummy's name as his password. She didn't know why, but it made her feel a bit funny inside. She was about to burst into tears when she noticed that the whole room had gone quiet.

She turned and saw all the scientists staring at her. They looked very startled.

'It's a little girl!' said one of them.

'A little Victorian girl!' said another.

'She's not supposed to be in here,' said a third.

'We should hand her in to Sir Digby Snottington,' said a fourth.

'Quick – grab her!' shouted a fifth.

And some of them began to approach her.

Ooh help, thought Tilly. *I've got to get out of here before they catch me and hand me over to Sir Digby Snotface.* She went to press the big green button marked GO . . . But it wasn't in her hand! She'd left it in the office! On the desk!

Some of the scientists were getting quite close. She had to escape. And just then she had a brainwave.

At the top of her voice she began singing

'**Shake** Your **Bum** Around'

and started doing spinning circles as she made her way towards the office. One step, two steps, spinning to the left, one step, two steps, spinning to the right she went.

'**Wiggle** your **bottom!**'

she sang as the startled scientists backed away, not knowing what was happening.

'Shake it up and down,
Just shake your bum,'

she wailed, flailing her arms even more than usual, for maximum effect. She was pleased to see her Victorian skirt and petticoats fanning out as she spun round, making her look bigger than she was.

The scientists were very confused. They didn't know what to do; it was hard to grab her when she was spinning all the time.

'Shake it to the left,
Wiggle your bottom,'

she carried on as they all looked on with their mouths hanging open. Some of them crouched down and hid behind their desks. And one began to cry.

This is working even better than it does in the High Street, thought Tilly.

'Shake it to the right,
My bum is fun!'

she bellowed as she reached the door of the office and ran in. She dashed over to the desk, picked up the button, pressed it – and immediately disappeared.

CHAPTER

Tilly found herself back in the kitchen at home. At first she thought she was exactly where she'd started, but then she realized that everything was just a little bit different.

On the fridge door she could see the message that had appeared in the photograph:

press f9

screen says reset

press y for yes

type password

mydar lingju lia

On the kitchen table there was a pile of balloons and two birthday cards – one that said

HAPPY 6TH BIRTHDAY

and another that said **6 TODAY!** from her aunty Helen.

And on the kitchen counter next to the sink she could see the birthday cupcake cake that her mummy had made for her sixth birthday. It looked absolutely scrumptious, but one cupcake was missing. The one with a T on, from the beginning of her name, had gone.

Tilly soon understood that she had gone back in time to her sixth birthday, and that the missing cupcake must be the one her dad had brought back with him, the one she'd eaten earlier that morning.

Was it earlier that morning? She'd been to so many places in so many times, and seen so many things. It was all very confusing.

Just at that moment her dad came into the

kitchen. 'Oh, Tilly, my darling angel, my darling, darling girl.' He ran over and clasped her in his arms. 'You made it!' he said. 'I thought I might have lost you forever.'

'Yes,' said Tilly, hugging him tightly. She was so pleased to see him, and so keen to tell him everything that had happened, that she ended up talking very fast, and it all came out in one big jumble. 'A man with a moustache came, and some big men tried to steal it, and then the fireworks went off, and then the machine stopped working, and then

I accidentally broke off the green button, and I
saw Admiral Nelson winning the World Cup with
Queen Victoria up a chimney. And then . . .' She
paused. 'And then . . . I went to where you work
and I saw all the pictures of Mummy in your
cupboard! And I never knew! And it made me
so happy. And I wish we could have pictures of
Mummy all over the house. Please can
we have them?
Please.'

'Of course we can, my angel. Of course we can. I'm sorry, we should have done it before, but I thought it would make you sad.'

'I didn't want to ask because I thought it would make *you* sad,' said Tilly.

They held each other very tight. Looking over her dad's shoulder, Tilly could see her birthday cupcake cake sitting on the kitchen counter.

'Are we actually home *now*?' she asked.

'We're sort of home,' her dad replied. 'But we're at home in the past. We're at home on your sixth birthday.'

'I thought so,' said Tilly. And then she asked rather timidly, 'Is Mummy here?'

'Yes,' said her dad rather carefully. 'And I've told her all about the time machine, so she knows we're not here for long.'

'But where is she?' asked Tilly.

'Here I am, Tilly,' came a voice from behind her.

Tilly spun round. It was her mummy. She was standing in the doorway.

'Mummy!'

Tilly ran to her. Her mummy picked her up in her arms and squeezed and squeezed and squeezed. Tilly buried her face in her mummy's neck. They were both crying tears of joy. Tilly's mummy smelled of peaches and honey. Tilly had almost forgotten the smell, but she knew now that she'd never forget it again.

Eventually her mummy said, 'Let me have a look at you.' And Tilly leaned back. 'My, look how you've grown. And you've got two new front teeth. And look at these ringlets, and this funny dress, and these petticoats. You look like a little Victorian girl. But you're still my little Tilly.'

Tilly wanted to say that she wasn't little, and that she was average height for her age, but she decided not to. Instead she said, 'Yes, I'm still your little Tilly.'

Tilly's mummy was feeling quite poorly and she had to sit down. But Tilly cheered her up by telling her all about her adventures with the time machine – about the rotary clothes line and the World Cup and the chimney sweeps. She told her all about going to the research centre, and about finding the pictures of her in Dad's cupboard, and about the password, and about singing

'Shake Your Bum Around'

and doing spinning circles. Her mummy and her

dad laughed and laughed when she told them that
one of the scientists had started to cry.

They had cups of tea and cupcakes, and they
were having such a good time that Tilly asked
if they couldn't just stay at her sixth birthday
forever.

But her dad said, 'It's out of our hands. Every
time we've pressed the button it has taken us to

another set of the coordinates that I programmed into the computer. I think the machine will probably take us back home to the present at any minute. It has just been waiting for us to be in the same time and place.'

'Why can't Mummy come with us? Why can't she be with us forever?' asked Tilly.

'That's the trouble with time machines,' said her dad. 'They can't always do what you want them to do.'

'But in a way I *will* always be with you,' said her mummy. 'If you try really hard to remember someone, it's a bit like being with them. And the thing is to try and remember them in a really happy way.'

She gave Tilly an extra-special squeeze. As Tilly squeezed her back, she thought she could hear the noise of the time machine in the distance. It was like a high-pitched whine mixed with a steady rumble and an electric hum, and it was getting louder and louder.

'I think it's happening,' said her dad. 'I think the time machine is taking us back to the present.'

Tilly leaned back so that she could see her mummy, but her mummy was beginning to disappear. First she started to look a little blurred, and then she slowly became more and more see-through.

'Try to remember all the happy times,' said her mummy, smiling an enormous smile, her voice becoming fainter and fainter. 'That way we'll always be together.'

'I will, I really will,' said Tilly as the noise of the time machine grew to a great crescendo.

And then suddenly everything stopped, the noise cut out, and Tilly and her dad were back in the present, in the kitchen. It was the same kitchen, except that her mummy wasn't there, nor were the cupcakes, or the balloons, or the birthday cards.

Tilly and her dad looked at each other in

silence for a while. It was as if the world was standing still.

They were both thinking about everything that had happened to them, and about what Tilly's mummy had said – that remembering someone was almost like being with them – and slowly but surely they both started smiling enormous smiles, just like her mummy.

'Right, young lady,' said her dad. 'I think it's time we made some changes around here. Let's get out the photo albums and find some lovely pictures of Mummy to put up on the walls.'

And they rushed towards each other and he scooped Tilly up into his arms. She hugged her dad so tightly that she could smell the burnt bits of his beard.

It felt like the sadness had suddenly gone out of their lives, and they were so full of love and joy that they actually started laughing. They laughed and laughed and laughed until tears were rolling down their faces.

CHAPTER

The first day after half-term Tilly was back at school. It was 'Dress as a Victorian' day, and Tilly won first prize for her 'frilly mushroom' outfit.

'Your dad even managed to put ringlets in your hair!' said Miss Scarborough, who was quite surprised at the lengths Tilly and her dad must have gone to, making all the clothes. 'And all these lace petticoats are very fine indeed.'

Tilly's best friend, Jack, won second prize for coming as a chimney sweep. She had told him that the most important thing was to make himself as dirty as possible, so Jack had rolled in all the dirt and grime he could find. He was

absolutely filthy, and everywhere he went
he left a trail of mud and soot. Eventually Miss
Scarborough asked him to sit in the corner so as
not to get the classroom too dirty.

Tilly also wrote a long story about what it
would have been like to be a chimney sweep in
Victorian times. Everyone in her class agreed that
it was very realistic, though Miss Scarborough

said that her invention of a man called Mr Wormwood was 'a bit far-fetched'.

Tilly made a change to her drawing of 'Afternoon Tea'. She added some party sausages on sticks. She told Miss Scarborough that she was 'absolutely certain' that Queen Victoria would have liked the idea.

Her dad picked her up from school, even though he was back at work. Apparently Sir Digby Snottington had written a very rude letter to the minister, and had been forced to resign. Tilly's dad was offered Sir Digby's old job as head of department. He told them he would only do it if he was allowed to drop Tilly off at school in the morning, and stop work in time to pick her up again in the afternoon. They had agreed because he was such a brilliant scientist.

The time machine was taken to the laboratory, and all the other scientists looked at it in wonder. They were very jealous. One of them was so jealous he started crying.

Tilly's dad spent most of his research time with the machine trying to locate a man called Mr Wormwood in 1887. When he eventually found him, he bought his watch back for £100, which was an enormous amount of money in Victorian times.

But best of all, in Tilly's mind, were the pictures of her mummy that were now all over the house. There was one in every room, though she still kept her old framed photo of her with her mummy and her dad on her bedside table.

CHAPTER

17

Tilly woke up with a start. At first she didn't know whether what she'd heard was part of a dream or something that had happened in real life. But she'd just heard a very

loud bang.

She lay under her duvet looking this way and that, trying to see things in her dark bedroom. She really wanted to find out what had made the noise, but it was a freezing cold night and she really didn't want to get out of bed.

Suddenly, through the gap in her thin curtains,

she saw a shower of sparks, which lit up her tiny bedroom. It was as if someone had set off a large firework just outside her window. In the light of the sparks she could see Big Tedder and Mr Fluffybunny sitting on the shelf at the end of her bed. She could also see her uniform laid out on the chair behind the door, ready for school in the morning. And she could see the big photo of her with her mummy and her dad, which she kept in a frame on her bedside table.

There was another bang, much smaller this time, followed by another shower of sparks. Tilly sniffed the air with her tiny button of a nose. Could she smell burning? She would have to get up and investigate.

She slid out of bed, dragging the duvet with her, wrapping it round her like a lovely warm cloak. She shuffled across to the window and looked out.

In the middle of the back yard she could see her dad. In front of him, upside down on the

ground, was his old bike. He was wearing black safety goggles which were slightly cracked, and holding a long metal stick that was attached to two gas canisters. When he pressed the metal stick against his bike it gave off a shower of sparks.

'What are you doing, Dad?' asked Tilly.

'Oh, hello, sweetpea. I'm sorry – did I wake you? I'm just fixing my bike. One of the forks needed welding,' he said. 'Nearly finished. Just got to get some PolyLube from the shed. You get back to bed. I promise I won't make any more noise.'

As her dad walked towards the shed, Tilly closed the window and the curtains. She dragged her duvet back on to her bed and climbed in.

Such a lot of things had happened in the last few days that sometimes she wondered if it hadn't all been a dream. Had her dad really invented a time machine? Had she really gone back in time to her sixth birthday? Had she really scared off the men who were trying to steal the time machine? And been on a pirate ship? And scored the winning goal for England? And met Queen Victoria?

Sometimes she wondered if it was all too good to be true.

She kissed the photograph of her with her mummy and her dad, turned off the light and snuggled down to go back to sleep.

But something was bothering her. Something was different.

She turned the light back on and looked at the photo. There she was on the morning of her sixth birthday, with her two front teeth missing. There was her mummy holding her tight and laughing, and there was her dad, pulling his funny squinty-eyed face. The one he always pulled.

But something was different. And then she saw it. It was the fridge in the background. All the usual stuff that was stuck to the fridge had gone. Instead, in magnetic letters, there was a message that read:

DANNY NOBLE is a comic-making, storytelling, ink-based illustrator who regularly falls off stages with her band the Meow Meows. By day she wrangles five-year-olds and sharpens pencils. She grew up by the sea with the most obscenely patient and wonderful family and now she lives in the city and swims with ducks.

TIME-TRAVELLER TRIVIA

It's time to test your time-travelling knowledge about some of the characters Tilly met on her adventure! Answers are at the end of the quiz.

1. As well as losing the sight in his right eye, which body part did Nelson lose?

A) His arm

B) His big toe

C) His right ear

2. How many grandchildren did Queen Victoria have?

A) 12

B) 42

C) 75

3. How old was William Pitt the Younger when he became Britain's youngest prime minister?

A) 36

B) 16

C) 24

4. When did England win the Football World Cup?

A) 1966

B) 1891

C) 2015

5. Who did England beat to win the Football World Cup?

A) Poland

B) West Germany

C) Brazil

6.
What was Queen Victoria's husband called?

A) Prince Albert

B) Lord Roger

C) Earl Ferdinand

Trivia answers: 1A, 2B, 3C, 4A, 5B, 6A

MAKE A TIME CAPSULE!

A time capsule is a box that you bury for people in the future to find. Inside the box you can put lots of things from your life that show what it's like to live in the twenty-first century!

What would you put in your time capsule?

What dates would you add to the timeline?

4 MAY 2017	*Tilly and the Time Machine* blasts into bookshops
24 MARCH 2015	Adrian Edmondson first tweets Danny Noble
29 JUNE 2007	Apple releases the iPhone
30 JULY 1966	England wins the World Cup
20 JUNE 1837	Queen Victoria comes to the throne
12 JULY 1794	Lord Admiral Nelson loses sight in his right eye
1651	Macaroons invented
150-100 B.C.E.	First gear-driven, precision clockwork machine

**If you had a time machine,
where would you go?
Fill in the blanks to write your own story!**

_____ AND THE TIME MACHINE

If I had a time machine, I'd travel to _____

so that I could meet _____.

Together we would eat lots of _____.

Then we would go to _____

to see the _____.

After that we would journey back to the present

and I would show _____ all the

amazing modern technology like _____.

Then we would eat some more _____

and write a book about our adventures.

Your story starts here . . .

Do you **love books** and
discovering new stories?
Then **www.puffin.co.uk**
is the place for you . . .

- Thrilling adventures, fantastic fiction
  and laugh-out-loud fun

- Brilliant videos featuring your favourite authors
  and characters

- Exciting competitions, news, activities,
  the Puffin blog and SO MUCH more . . .